BOSTON
CASUALTY

BOSTON
CASUALTY

TEN STORIES & VARIATIONS

DAVID TAYLOR JOHANNESEN

Print information available on the last page.

Rev. date: 04/23/2019

To order additional copies of this book, contact:
Xlibris
1-888-795-4274
www.Xlibris.com
Orders@Xlibris.com
786197

CONTENTS

—an eternal city its Commonwealth doth embrace
unto a wond'rous saving, a hallowed place,
where none may come forward to disgrace
or put upon a preternatural face—

Foreword

I shall explain my reason for the title, *Boston Casualty*, and with it to express my lament at the demise of the fishing stocks in the waters by the great fleet of New Bedford, Massachusetts. While haddock remain plentiful, cod and flounder are badly depleted. Having grown up in Boston, and maintained a residence and sailboat in South Dartmouth, in Buzzards Bay, I am greatly grieved.

Descending down a narrow street from the State House we arrived at a small, recently re-furbished hotel with an old engraved stone at the entrance which read Boston Casualty. The structure had been occupied by an insurance company a century before. Ensuing events in the Commonwealth have prompted perhaps an ironic view of the title. And, as I presently live in Los Angeles, I shall allow myself a broad license in that direction Imagined.

We shall not cease from exploration, and the end of all our exploring, will be to arrive where we started and know the place for the first time.

—T.S. Eliot

About the Author

David Taylor Johannesen was born in Salt Lake City and grew up in Boston. His earlier published literary works are:

Tales of Love and Valor, Two Novellas (2018)
Falcons and Seagulls, a Utah Tale (2015)
Last One Close the Gate, Selected Stories (2012)
*Vespers East & West, Selected Poems (2011)**

*Written at Oxford, 1996

Johannesen lives in Los Angeles with his life Linda and border collie Fallon. His ancestry is Scottish and Norwegian. He was educated at University of Pennsylvania, New York University and Oxford University, U.K.

Johannesen has two children: a son, Christian, a media executive in New York City; and a daughter, Helen, a restaurateur and sommelier in Los Angeles.

Immaculate Heart

When I came to California from life-long tributaries of New England, I immediately enrolled myself in a Catholic retreat house in Montecito beside the San Yisidro Creek at the foothills of the Los Padres National Forest. I had been pleasantly plagued with a dissociative condition in which, for extended swaths of time, I thought of and heard myself as two different people—a confusion, perhaps, of what my Boston psychiatrist dismissed as a 'misalignment' of my *Alpha & Omega* spheres of personality—as if I were trading places recklessly with what my twin sister saw as my male and female firmaments. At the retreat house, I fell into a space supplied and consecrated by the kind sisters, novitiates of an order I cannot recall, and I let my Quaker bones subside in their grace, for I had no other recourse for the missteps or even bald confusion I had found and abruptly and foolishly discarded: I foundered on my own petard as my grandfather once said.

It is five thirty; Centering Prayer in the library has just ended and the guests will soon gather at six for dinner downstairs in the Great Hall. I sat at a desk in front of a huge casement in one of the second-story rooms of the vast, mission-style house watching the dusk begin to apply a salmon brushstroke across the Channel Islands twenty miles out to sea from Santa Barbara. Once a private residence, its quarried sandstone walls are surrounded by twenty-six acres of giant live-oaks, avocado trees, orange groves, flowering acacias, eucalyptus and alders—drawing me into a new rewoven pattern in my life—new surroundings I could recognize and embrace within my old life.

This weekend was my third such retreat after coming to California to marry. The year before, I had begun to explore time at the Sanctuary—or, rather, to allow myself access to a vestibule of faith where past and future were separate spheres—their immanence pouring over the present as if it were an adopted child—not as ends of a linear cord upon which the present is the main dimension. In this way, I visited my mother before she died, when I was a child of five; gave my daughter in marriage six years hence; and listened to conversations with recent contemporary colleagues in other times in our thirty-year careers—: *Othertimers,* I called people I knew, or encountered in the same place, usually, but in a different time. Naturally, visions of time as existing in multiple spectrums were not new, and I pretended merely a glancing knowledge of physics—and knew that time travel, with or without the curve of light, had held the interest of science fiction writers and readers for a century, since H.G. Wells. Nor did I ever align my beliefs with auguries performed by ancient civilizations such as the Celts, who would sleep after eating the flesh of ritually sacrificed animals, and in their dreams seek knowledge about the future from their ancestors. The Vikings may have eaten each other for a glimpse of whatever they thought time represented for them: unlikely!

"Today I had an *othertime* experience walking my two dogs on the beach," I announced at the dinner table the second night of the retreat. A complement of eight guests was present at table and turned in hopeful tolerance towards me. "You may have seen my black and white collies in the kennels out back. Well, I decided to give them a run on the beach near the See the Sea Motel—it's a lovely, mile-long arc between two long breachways—down close to San Ysidro and the freeway. From the exact opposite end of the beach, two identical Border collies—one male and one female, like mine, one small and one good-sized with the same markings—came trotting toward me yards ahead of their owner, a man of my age and height also wearing rolled-up khaki pants, like mine!"

"Perhaps the very ones you are wearing now," observed Sister Pat, one of the four nuns who cooked and joined us for dinner. "I noticed they are wet at the cuffs—but no sand seems to have come into the House."

"Oh, dear, I hope I didn't bring any sand inside—yet you assure me, Sister Pat, bless you—I washed my feet or, to be truthful, I watched the other man on the beach wash his feet in the sea and put on tennis shoes before he took his dogs away—they trotted off, looking back as my own."

"Where are your dogs now?" Sister Pat continued, having rescued the others from the obligation to attend Solomon, not one of their own—not because he had not been before and they remembered him, but due to a distance he carried in his smile, his off-handed way, and tailored suit.

"I believe, as I wonder, that they're somewhere in the future."

"Are they back in the kennel, behind the house?" she probed.

"Well, yes, they jumped out of the back of the Jeep in the same way they always do, but ran around through the orange trees. I called, but—"

"—they took a different path?" she surmised penitently, aware with assurance I could not ignore.

"Yes, sister Pat. But when I was opening the kennel door for them, I was immediately opening the door to the dining room, here! I simply stepped from one to the other, and here I am—no dogs, no kennel—"

"I'm sure they're somewhere around, and they're fine. We'll look for them after dinner—they could be chasing small animals, even coyotes up in the woods. You simply had a *lapse in faith,* or a moment of grace when you move through the Holy Spirit to the place you imagine where you belong." Sister Pat bent towards our meal of turkey loaf, boiled carrots and salad.

"*Coyotes?*" I gasped, thinking of them waiting in packs. A very pretty, Irish, sort of reddish-blonde woman sitting next to me took my hand under the frail lace tablecloth. We had only met briefly after Centering Prayer, and had chatted amiably as we walked together in the broad meadow encircling a large vegetable garden the sisters tended all year.

"I'm Mary Beatrice," she told me as we left the

table together. "I've been here many times, but I don't remember you. Three years ago— it was the first time I came to Casa Maria—after my divorce, I was walking on the same beach and saw dogs just like yours. If we can take a walk after dinner, I'll tell you about it. Bring a flashlight. I know you're in one of the grand front rooms; you will find a flashlight—I am in one of the small, unheated alcoves at the back, no flashlights, only candles—*Solomon.*"

The other residents at the retreat were couples, two Anglican clergy and their spouses who were seeking to enrich their ministries, or enliven their marriages—I was not able to decide even by sounds in the wall—and a middle-aged woman who painted in her room and was seen only at meals. The last was an elderly man who played the ancient piano in the drawing room, darkly hooded with worn tapestries floor-to-ceiling and draperies faded in decades from puce to taupe, even at sunset when the light fell across the old man's hands withered into Schubert and Mozart. That made eight guests at a table for twelve including the four sisters.

"Mary Beatrice," I marveled as we stepped outside and my flashlight sought the dim perimeter of the grounds. "Both holy names."

"Mary, I know," she blushed. "Beatrice was my mother's sister."

"Beatrice? An angel of Dante and Shakespeare!" I cried in the dark, as I gathered her tiny waist in my arm, feeling myself blessèd.

"I don't know about that, but I'm sure you'll teach me— *about both.*"

"Let's walk around to where the kennels are supposed to be," I said as she took my hand from her waist and pressed it against her cheek. We found a small path, a serpentine around the great house I had not seen during my initial tramping over the vast property only yesterday—*was it?*

"Listen: I can hear your dogs very close," she whispered, "whimpering in their absolute loyalty to you. Do you hear them? Soon they'll be yelping for you, to give you direction, then they'll bark to scold you for leaving—"

"But I never left them," I turned sharply to assure her, even hoping to kiss her, finally, but she had gone, left my arm without a touch and re-tracing her steps without a footfall for me to follow, or imagine. Now I heard the dogs barking as she had; I crawled over a path to let them find my scent.

"They never go anywhere without me!" I gasped back at Beatrice. She was nowhere near me, yet I still felt the hand of *Paradisio* on my cheek and every moment since dinner was as differentiated as the stars, light years ago extinguished but still showing their afterlives—even the moment she and I left suddenly before the blueberry tart and ice cream had been set before us. I turned back to the path we had taken, watching for the dogs and watching for her. At the wide, circle drive in front of the house I bent to fit my key in the lock, not seeing my cuffs were filled with sand and my jeep was no longer parked in its place

Upstairs, Solomon hesitates at the junction of two long,

paneled halls. His room is two doors to the right; the other rooms lay four doors on the left, where the corridor was much longer and led to the small chapel and to the cold, back alcove where Mary Beatrice slept, between the chapel and the back stair. The chapel overlooks an open terrazzo below, which forms the center of the house. So there were eight large bedroom suites at the front of the second floor, and the chapel and rooms for the sisters at the back. Perhaps Beatrice had meant she was lodged in one of the former servants' rooms from days gone by—but that was where sisters lived! Was she staying in a secret, even imaginary chamber, with no heat? He decides to investigate that area and opens a door into the chapel. At this late hour it was quiet, with only a line of votive candles lighting the sidewalls to show there was the nearness of a service ended, or ahead.

Mass and Centering Prayer are held here, as well as brief prayers of intercession, petitions offered, each chorale ending God hear our prayer. For two evenings, Solomon had nothing to ask for: his parents were long dead in the sinking of Andrea Doria after a collision in 1956 off Nantucket and his grown children were happy and flourishing He sat quietly in his chair. Now he is holding an orange Beatrice picked for him hours before, digging his nails into its pulp as a gesture of atonement, he thinks, and then sees several people not seen before—certainly not at dinner, or in the Common Room—file in behind Sister Pat with solemn purpose.

"Excuse me—I was just looking, sitting really, in the silence—" he thought to say, remembering his Quaker upbringing in Massachusetts.

"Solomon, please join us," Sister Pat entreated as she faced the alter.

"I'm looking for Mary Beatrice," he told her plainly. "Isn't her room nearby? And—have you seen my dogs? They weren't in their kennel when I went out after dinner—and Mary Beatrice and I heard them barking!"

"Don't worry about them now—they're safe. We're here for you!" He sees the glow of her skin, a lambent pink he had before judged to her being overweight, perhaps suffering from high blood pressure. But her face is clear and roseate, the hue of an excited child rushing up to present herself after play, in anticipation of praise and delight. The blood rushes innocently into the capillaries of her faith, and not from illness: fulfilled.

"You spoke to us about time at dinner this evening," she continued. "What do we know about God's plan? We're all on a path. We're about to walk what we call the Labyrinth in this chapel—not unlike labyrinthine wanderings man has done since the ancient Greeks, and before. You will see the markings on our modest floor leading each of us to Jerusalem—"

"But I have been to Jerusalem, the land many times, and in my heart as I always looked for the New Jerusalem which I have found in William Blake, and Susana of the Wells—and now, unexpectedly, in Mary Beatrice!"

"There is no Mary Beatrice with us here. Yes, Sister Mary and Sister Beatrice are both of our order. They are in their rooms now; they have their devotions after dinner. You will not see them until breakfast. Is it possible you have combined them into one person you once knew, or as a transformative act of reverence to the mission we follow?"

"But my Beatrice was with us at dinner, and walked with me in your meadows, and led me to the kennels to wait for my dogs to return, and assured me of so much more than their return: We formed a covenant—"

"Which should lead you into a higher place of knowing who she is!"

"Then, tell me Sister Pat: What year is this? My calendar says 1989."

"No, dear Solomon. It is the year of our Lord 2002, and you're here."

"I can't be here, and if I am, I am in the wrong place I expected life to bring me to—I left so much behind as excess baggage to be with you—"

"But you had no idea of what you were leaving behind and what you are looking for," Sister Pat insisted. "You have no idea of where you are!"

"Then, I had best go back to my room and prepare to leave. My dogs are near, and Mary Beatrice has vanished from my struggling heart—"

Again in the face of these entreaties, I backed away from the chapel—its low arched ceilings brushed with the light of many candles, reflected a whorl of faces and names I wished I could recover. Some—there were ten altogether—had become familiar in two days, perhaps from my last retreat, the day after Thanksgiving when I had eaten cold turkey legs and dressing with my wife on the Zuma beach at Malibu. Some ancient, warring spirit had driven me into to the ocean, and I badly misjudged a huge rogue wave, which threw me into unconsciousness for a few moments. My face was dragged raw, mouth and ears filled with sand as my shoulders slammed into the firmament of the shore, which took me to a vision of my death, yet I still loved to swim in cold waters to feel my iced head throb free.

I opened the door to my room, a sanctuary offering a bathroom of magenta tile and a tub set and inlaid with black and fuchsia mosaic tiles in the late 1920's and early 1930's when the house was built by three successive owners. I pushed the heavy carved oak door shut. The dark gave way to a single light burning beside the massive bed. I could pack a few belongings in an instant and leave this life and time behind—my toothbrush, razor, jeans and two flannel shirts. No—one flannel shirt: I had given the other to Mary Beatrice after our walk together after dinner.

I felt I was throwing my life into a very small knap-sack, remains of what was not left on a trail, but had dreaded to take with me—a fabric of regret as tightly woven as the seams of my sleeping bag and tent I had brought with me, not knowing what to expect for accommodations—with whom to share.

"I am here for you, Solomon of the ancients," she called softly from beneath the counterpane on the bed. "Where have you been, my savior—?"

"Are you an angel, or two angels? Why haven't I found you before?"

"I am your angel tonight—" a slender coil of past remembrance came from her voice, a distance of no more than half a breath, half a life halved again—:

"Do I pray to you or may I make love to you?" he resisted and released his last memory of her not long before, her hand upon his cheek, now a fist.

"You will find out when you crawl under these covers and warm my toes, to begin with, and then promise me you have come back from that disturbing absence from time you set before us and pulled us under for the past two days—and I cannot calculate how many years you've lost."

"Who is *us* you throw about as if I know the characters you've found to stand in place of our own truth? Don't answer. Come into my arms—"

She had no answer as he entered her, and her arms and legs flayed back in joyful conviction—a real woman he feared as phantom, leading him astray—now a woman who had surrendered her anterior life and calling to the absolute truth of his loins, and hers, bound up in eternity.

Four Twins & A Wedding Dress

It may be some time before my memory may escort you into the gray, worn Spanish portals of *Bethesda by the Sea* Episcopal Church in Palm Beach where Lily and I were married following a sedulous yet sly courtship by our two fathers—both long-aligned law associates, separated by twenty years in age: hers, the young disciple pioneer out on Route 128; mine, the Boston lawyer guiding his protégé's inventions diligently through the *Scylla & Charybdis* of patents and wiles of venture financing. But I need first to take you back to the moment we first met, I as her godfather when she was five and then through her teens as I taught her to sail in Buzzards Bay on the South Coast of Massachusetts.

Lily, twenty, and an equal span of years younger than I, turned up in an American Literature class I was then teaching at Amherst College in western Massachusetts. Her father had encouraged her to take my class, and we knew each other from the first day when we struck our own friendship, had coffee after school and often joined our fathers for dinners in Back Bay.

After Lily arrived, I assigned the class Saul Bellow's *Henderson The Rain King*, a sly tale of a wealthy Connecticut man of fifty who flees to Africa to direct his discordant appetites for life towards one crowning purpose—that he might return home freed from rage. I chose the book because I myself had turned to teaching because of rage, and because Henderson's younger wife in the book is also called Lily—an association I failed to recognize at the time:

I came to believe both Lily the character and Lily my student might converge in some fugitive place where I could escape the calamities which had beset my life the year before—to be described in the pages ahead. That Lily, my daughter's age, may take me though a fictional embrasure, turned out to be improbable yet inevitable when she arrived in Palm Beach during the Amherst Spring vacation.

My daughter Diana arrived at the invitation of her grandfather. We all gathered at an Everglades Club dance, fathers beaming and daughters stupefied and I, newly divorced, driven under the table—so to speak—hiding behind the sleek and varied skirts of immense draperies, as I had been named her god-father twenty years before.

Lily and I danced happily after dinner, and I was surprised, perhaps not having noticed her standing to recite in the classroom that she was almost my height. Now I felt her strong, elastic carriage, her buoyancy turning her shoulders of pale alabaster and the long nape of her neck bending towards me. She took fast, certain steps to the old-fashioned music as if she had known it before I did. "I feel like I'm on a boat," she whispered. "I remember you teaching me sailing when I was twelve out on Buzzards Bay—"

"All the coffees we had together after class—do you feel well acquainted at least?" I asked at the same moment. She leaned backwards, as if adhering to an extravagant dance step I may have introduced, but stopped and put her arms casually behind her hips—which were suddenly and surprisingly wide even when surrendered to the fast-tapering, long legs which fell into slippers as narrow and constrained as a child's first ballet shoes—: she pulled up and let her arms droop over my shoulder.

"You are my teacher—yes? So teach me some new steps!"

I had no thought she was wooing me to the extent our fathers hoped for until late that night, after, the dance when back in my room. It was connected by a large bathroom to my daughter Diana's room where Lily was staying: her father had house guests and no room for her, while my father had four bedrooms and no guests except my daughter. We swung open the sliding glass doors of my terrace to take in the damp, fecund breeze from the water-way mingled with the scents of cypress and black pepper trees and even jacarandas growing miles away. Just across the way, lights swam down the rigging of two or three-masted yachts at their moorings on the Intercoastal Waterway which flowed down from the Delaware.

"I may want to stay here with you," Lily told me quietly "—and Diana, of course."

The sounds of a small complacent orchestra rose from the hard, polished deck of one of these boats, the notes indistinct from one another in the thick wetted air, and Lily and I took up the elusive tune and danced again. She soon pushed me back, her arms braced over my shoulders so that I could look into her *mignonette* green eyes, flecked with the pallor of wandering and white changeable lights of her skin. For the first time since she came to my class six months before, we kissed. It was a forbearing kiss, saying, 'Hello, who are you? We've met before—' ahead of the sweep of passion which might make us recognize each other, or to recall her joking at one of our many coffee hours after class—"dad says you're forty: that's nothing! I am an old twenty, and there are *two of me*, two Lilys—"

"Two of you?" I marveled at her unfolding joke.

"I am a changeling who's taken my dead sister's place and her name! As you know, she died in a car crash when we were sixteen. Before you say anything, I'm taking a shower. Is there a robe in the bathroom? Is it too soon in our friendship to ask if you want to join me—is there a robe in the bath?"

"Mine. White terrycloth, with a hood for your hair," I could only stammer, and bless her for a hidden fidelity which had shown itself in the exquisite candor of dancing with me at the club. I could never have expected my narrow world to be touched any other woman. "I'll wait for you here," was all I said as I let go of her mane of auburn hair I had gathered. I only wanted, that night, to dry her hair, which would fall like a lashed willow moving in verdant sweeps—a frail, faint *verdoyant* dad would say—marking to my eyes innocence like a trail of discovery whose clues were larger than my own life. Divorced, broken, an author abandoned by his publisher, a screenwriter dropped by his producer, I stumbled upon the notion I could offer this girl a life—such was the sudden flair of intimacy which arose from the evening's innocent pleasures.

When she reappeared, bound in my old Harvard Alumni Club robe—whose faded crimson chevron looked

15

more like the twisted grin of an aging, mangy lion—she stretched on one of the twin rattan beds in my room. "I simply took my sister's place and name. I didn't want to be Rose anymore," she continued from where she had left off. He skin was colored the deep red of porphyry, as if gathered from within.

"Yes, of course. I remember you as Rose, Lily's twin. In class you were Lily. So, you're *legally* Lily?"

"Yes, but did your father, *or mine*—they were so *tight!*—tell you that he encouraged me to take Lily's name and to act as her surrogate? I even stepped in with her boyfriend who, dear heart, didn't learn of this until I went off to college two years later! And there I eventually landed in your sophomore class because my dad said I should study with you—his mentor's son—"

"That part, no. But I knew you were there. Your father is a big contributor to the school, and my father casually mentioned you were attending and I should look out for you—*whoever you are, you are my god-daugther!"* I leaned to kiss her lightly.

"So, we're betrothed, especially as I step into your room in a robe" she laughed almost seriously into my ear as I lay beside her, still in my evening clothes from the dance. "Don't you see, our fathers have long since given us their *permission.* They've had something of a *conclave* to ordain our marriage—although *we're* Jewish, so that term might not be the right world, but it will be a Christian—"

"And do you realize I picked *Henderson The Rain King* to study because I knew you, my god-daughter, were in the

16

class? Two Lilys, so much younger, so out-of-reach—could I have thought your sister was you—

"*Shut up and fuck Rose, if you must*—it's my first—" she whispered, opening herself and spreading out the robe to catch any blood." And her legs, long as mine pulled me utterly inside her so, that touching the oculus of her cervix, I knew, and she knew of a first beloved of many we were about to conceive.

"Solomon O Solomon, *husband*—" she cried and she swung herself above me, as if she were riding her horse, so I could watch her watching me in elegant, half-lidded equine authority, and bless her in return with my submission to her stewardship. From my avuncular experience of her in the classroom—off-handed exchanges in coffee houses and during our tramps in the Berkshire snows—I knew that she had never stood aside from her life as *Lily,* but over the weeks was introducing me to *Rose* and had invited me to taste the rare sobriquet at her core. But she pleaded—at first in the shadows conflated by water I thought she was asking me not to leave her, to give her a chance to be Rose again—:

"—Don't move, don't move," she admonished. And I settled into a slower method and a gentle release of what I am certain was the gestation of our first child, Nathaniel after my mother's great grandfather, the first Fairchild in New England. "I'm filled up and sore!" she cried, racing for the shower.

Two days later, we were racing in my father's 1966 Jaguar across Alligator Alley, one hundred miles of straight road across the Everglades. Lily sat in the back where she had folded down the fine- grained and silver-hinged walnut writing desks to address wedding invitations which seemed to flow from her pen as fast as the speedometer permitted. Her father, forsaking Palm Beach, lived in Naples, where *post-chase* we would have to select a wedding gown, photographers, caterers and a chamber orchestra associated with the performing arts center. Most guests would be invited by telephone

"I do like the Gulf Coast much more than your snobby *Gold Coast*," she quipped from behind me as she flicked my ears with close-sprung thumbs and middle fingers. I pushed the Jag to a hundred!

"It is odd, our fathers so close, they should live a hundred miles apart when they live a block away in Boston," I ventured to span the twenty years I had over her well-sharpened wisdom of family fugues.

According to a patriarch's prerogative, my father tip-toed into my room—*our room*—next and every morning with a breakfast tray: an enamel French pot with dark coffee and chicory, and glasses of hand-squeezed orange juice together with fresh hot *empañadas* from Rafael's musical, laughing kitchen.

"A Florida breakfast for the kids landed from the frozen deeps of the Berkshires!" he beamed. From the beginning, he gazed fondly at us as already married, established, coupled and planning children, wading through our small likes and dislikes and not at all embarrassed, our nuptials, still days away, had already been spent under his roof a room away from his arriving eighteen-year old granddaughter, the presumptive maid of honor. Even the first night, as Lily lay sleeping in my arms, I glanced at the night table to see my late mother's emerald & diamond engagement ring perched upon a tiny crimson velvet pillow, waiting for Lily's hand. I slipped it on her finger as she slept, and in the morning she wept, "*Oh, joy—*"

"But we've got to get cracking," he said. "Lily's dad wants to take us sailing up at Hobe Sound at noon—when the tide is in and the mullet are running—and wants to announce your engagement at the club up there. Many of his friends from Boston are there, quite a few of mine too if truth be told." At seventy, Harvard Law '52, he bowed out of the room elaborately, like an old retainer from Chekov, or as meekly as his servant and companion, Rafael, might approach and withdraw from the master suite, barefoot and singing, to accept his duties—although dad wore slippers and *Sulka* pajamas. Lily buried her head in the pillows to smother her laughter. I coiled with her beneath the counterpane. "Have you ever wondered about our two fathers?" she whispered.

"Wondered—how?" I came up for air and poured us each huge bowls of coffee and steamed milk, completing my father's French grandeur—I had only to look at his Braques on the wall to remember this—and pulled the tray close to her now primly folded legs as she sat up.

"Well, I remember my mother saying to me that when

she married my father, it was as if she married two men—your father was always with them, and forever *planning their lives.*"

"—and hasn't that turned out pretty well for everyone—?"

"It's not just that!" she pleaded, lacing her leg over mine beneath the covers and slowly raising her coffee to her mouth with both hands. "Isn't it strange that neither of them has expressed any reservation about our age difference? It seems they've printed invitations, planned this wedding and even pushed us together from the beginning. Of course I've loved you since the first week of classes, but still—"

"This is beginning to sound like a Gilbert and Sullivan opera—either that or something much more sordid which, if I may say so, you're too young to grasp the raw truth or falsehoods of—" I let my sarcasm slowly rise above my tenderness, something I could not have imagined doing to Lily—

"Hold on there, professor, you're not in class, and no one is going to sue you for breach-of-promise if you should decide not to marry me—pregnant as I already may be."

"Silly-filly, I'd be a fool to lose you—especially as you get on so well with Diana. Not every eighteen-year-old daughter of a divorced man would take to a replacement of her mother by someone nearly her age when she married!"

"If we can get back to our fathers...?" She leaned to kiss me, and pushed the tray further down the bed as she noticed how hard I was. She pulled me down to her and said, "Let's make *sure.* It's my perfect time of month—and shall we spell our first-born's name your Christian New England way, with i, e, l, or the Jewish style, Nathanael?" I kissed the question from her mouth, *my eternal Jewess!*

We forgot about our fathers for the next half-hour. Later in the morning I began to wonder about the quarter-century of dad's mentoring. Had it begun with an infatuation when hers was just out of law school, twenty-five, and mine, fifty years, was the sagacious, arising prominent lawyer then running for Governor of Massachusetts? My father had never remarried after my mother died, and even brought Rafael, his valet and driver in Boston and *my age,* down to Florida to live with him here. But hadn't Lily's father *found* Rafael to fill father's position? Idolatry? Sexual? *Homosexual—?* I forced back a shock of recognition like a dam denying a reservoir of origins.

"I bet I know where your febrile brain is going with this!"

"There's nothing *fevered* about my thinking, if that's what you mean, dear heart. As you know, I'm cold and lucid—and don't think I've forgotten how you-of-the-first-row tortured me with your games in vocabulary and syntax—"

"It wasn't a very 'cold and lucid' man with me under the sheets just now or, for that matter, who danced with me last night and wanted to swim naked with me in the ocean at two a.m.—no, I've never thought our fathers were once *lovers,* although their mutual connection to Rafael does suggest familiarity with a certain...*world?* You see, my dad did send Rafael down to live with yours."

"Are you kids up?" my father's soothing tones came through the door. "*Really!* It's past eleven, and we've got to be back from sailing for dinner at six. I'd like to stop at the inlet by the bridge and show you the running mullet. How was your breakfast?" he asked more timidly, a wandering feature of his large, commanding nature which emerged in submissive moments.

"Wonderful! We're up, and just going over the vows we might want Reverend Wilcox to read on Saturday," Lily called brightly as she kicked me and nearly the tray with Rafael's *empanadas* to the floor. "*What's his fascination with mullet—?*"

"Vows? What vows? Isn't old Wilcox providing them?"

"Not exactly, dad," I put in somberly as Lily fled into the bathroom. "There will be some of the usual Anglican stuff, we adding some passages from the *Siddur* to honor Lily's Judaism. Her dad must have mentioned it to you?"

"He may have," my father pondered, now in our bedroom fully studying the detritus of breakfast, threshed bedclothes and flung-aside evening clothes against the wavering light trying to pour in through closed draperies. "But Frederick was long ago, still now, given to lapses in his attention, but I am delighted—for his sake—that you have amended your nuptials. Now, Tuesday next, the supper in your honor is being given by retired Judge Haddock of the Massachusetts Supreme Court, a dear friend, colleague, and, if I may say, a mentor-*ajoint* with me for Lily's dear father. Since we are not doing a 'rehearsal' dinner due to Friday being the Hebrew Sabbath, the judge and Lily's father decided on next week: nearly fifty people will be attending, many flying down from Boston." He seemed in a pre-nuptial frenzy—:

For it was as if my father had read a legal brief, or a rapt, closing summation in court he had pinned to an epaulet on my shoulder, awarding me a mark of distinction that I had perhaps *understood him,* and would offer no rebuttal or modification of his intent. Lily sang in the shower in a way that made my father suddenly glow: *a grandchild? Oh, name him after Joclyn, please.*

He reached for our breakfast tray and turned away to return it to Rafael's kitchen—embarrassed perhaps that we had not touched the *empanadas*—just as Lily emerged from the bathroom in her, *Lily's,* extravagant cotton robe with a bleached, straggling chevron on its chest from the beach club, and kissed my father's nape for hope of a distant legacy.

"All is well, then," he smiled at her. "Shall we leave in a half hour? We'll take route A-1-A all the way, to see the mullet flee."

The wedding—two weeks later—as I promised—: Before over one hundred guests, Reverend Wilcox proclaimed the sanctity of our union. A rabbinical student, a niece of Lily's father, had written, and read out the promises of our *Ketuba.* We were to be soul-mates to each other, *as beloveds and friends,* to share all in love. So we emerged with two legal contracts of marriage: one, from the State of Florida—an absurd notion to us both—; and the other a script as sublime as common sense. Lily read a poem of Emily Dickinson—I promised to read T.S. Eliot's: *We shall not cease from exploration, and the end of all our exploring will be to arrive where we started and know the place for the first time—*

The reception, from which our two fathers vanished midway, was lavish and enclosed in the cloistered ground of *Bethesda-by-the Sea.* Guests were not primarily from Florida, although our fathers had gathered many friends from their *sojourns des Sud* over the years. More, though we were not certain, came from New England, irritable but correct in their summons to such a foreign land. Lily's classmates—my *other* students!—swam currents; our living aunts and uncles, cousins and even three of my writing friends and even my agent from Los Angeles thronged as happily as nascent moons of Jupiter seeking, never finding, an orbital alternative.

"Solly—when are you coming back to writing screenplays?" one of them asked querulously. "We need you back—" my agent nodded in sly contempt.

"Never: I am pledged to a life I have never lived, and drawn to a freedom I never imagined. With this woman's forbearance and my own forgiveness—I'll last forever! Hollywood can go fuck itself!" Yet—

"What was *that* all about?" my bride whispered as we walked along the cloistered passage flanking the outside of the church. "Rather a tall order, isn't it—especially for me! In two short sentences have you proclaimed a new

24

life—and lot of lovely *work* for me—or is it the manic excitement of us settling into your lovely cottage near Amherst?" she rolled the words with an impertinence which pulled me up short, but was adorable.

"How about California?" the words stumbled out of me. "I still have a roomy bungalow in Topanga Canyon—warm winters?"

"Topanga," she repeated, her compliant humor dimming like a harbor vaporing with morning fog.

"Yes—: It winds in from the ocean near Malibu, then through a grubby little village and ends ten miles later at Calabasas, in the 'Valley'. My house is in the middle and high up—nearly two thousand feet. Live oaks, sage, even yarrow—"

"Do you truly want to go back to work in...*Hollywood?* What about your teaching? Sailing out to Falmouth? The *Commonwealth!*"

"Maybe we can do both: Spend the winter in Topanga and add summer classes at Amherst. No more snow for my expecting angel, and I only need three months in L.A.—"

"Darling, I *like* snow! I love winter in New England, don't you? We both grew up there, I want us to go cross-country skiing—especially if I'm pregnant—"

"But I can take you cross-country skiing ninety minutes north of Los Angeles, in the Los Padres Mountains—think of it—so many climates to find!"

"I'm thinking that you're a very lucky boy because I'll love you wherever, and *whenever we are.* If you want to get back to your writing—and from your west-of-the-west friends at the wedding I can imagine your contacts out there—I'll be your biggest fan! And think of it: for half the year or more you'll be teaching me in class at Amherst, and for the rest of the time you'll write for me, won't you? And our baby born at home, in Massachusetts, where our fathers and cousins are. And a drive across the country—however can we manage that?" She wailed as a great unknown landscape beset her.

She faltered as I teased her with a jingle of keys in my pocket and she dove to find the sound's provenance. "The Jag!" she let out almost an empyrean appeal to the Gods.

"Dad has given it to us. It's a classic, over twenty-five years old, perfectly maintained and running on its third engine. We can set out at Christmas break—taking the southern route, naturally, and be in LA in six days—"

"You're the classic!" she cried. "You're my antique!"

I kissed her as I had not found suitable after our vows in church. Her inordinate dress billowed in a sudden wind and flew into my arms—an embrasure holding somewhere a tiny creature just beyond my finger tips—my wife shyly, swiftly emerging from this spun lace and silk sanctuary.

"Who am I," she laughed indulgently, "to restrain your powers—and you mine? I am everything you need, and nothing without you—a very simple, exquisite match, and we should leave after Thanksgiving to be back by—"

"—May first, so I can prepare for my classes and you can present...*bambino molto bene, ma non troppo!* And I'll say another thing: I'm glad we live at the other end of the Commonwealth from Boston—*from our fathers*—and when we're down on the South Coast in my grandmother's house we're with my sister who I saw you talking to a lot at the wedding—laughing your heads off. And you'll get to love my twin, Leah"

"Yes, Solly: I was amused to hear from her how you Fairchild children were named Solomon and Leah, from the Old Testament—after your father's parents. Solomon *Redux* and Leah *Redux* Fairchild. Indeed! You never told me what your middle initial, *R,* stood for. *Redux!*" She elbowed me aside.

"So you married a re-tread, with a twin-sister re-tread. Our parents' slack joke—although I've been told my poor mother resisted it—borne aloft by my father's wry, persuasive, predatory nature. Face it: he *controlled your father!*"

"Well...you have just married *two Lily's*—you're a *bigamist!* And I know that's not funny, but twins constantly invent and reinvent themselves mainly to remain *part of each other* as they grow older, and if one dies the other is obligated to assume the identity and *assure the safety of the departed spirit.*" She watched me closely to be certain I understood.

"But you don't *portray* two personalities—even if you have...adopted some part of your sister's—unless I've missed something, in which case I fell in love with both of you. So, I have either a forty-year old wife, or two aged twenty. It's suddenly time to go to the reception: I'll dance with *both of you—Lilys!*"

The urge to try on Lily's wedding dress—followed by the plan to have it altered in the waist only, as she was nearly my height—came over me like the newly sprung moon rising over the Inter-coastal Waterway the night after our reception. Perhaps wearing the family kilt, a Liang/Fairchild tartan, at the wedding, and Lily finding it so sexy dancing against my bare legs at the reception gave me the exegesis to calmly and rationally explore this urge.

It was very late, and Lily and my daughter Diana were in her room giggling and finishing a last bottle of champagne they had taken from the reception. I was sleepy, having been sailing all morning in rough seas off Hobe Sound with the owner of the boat we were to sail in the next day to Key Largo for our honeymoon. Earlier, when we got home, Rafael joked that he'd like to look under my kilt to be certain I wore no underwear—encouraged from the sidelines by my father, barely awake. Lily proclaimed that this a hidden truth only she was allowed to discover—"if I don't know already!" Rafael soon dutifully put father to bed and Lily did the same with me after slowly, with mock-fugitive shyness, drawing off the kilt and asserting her own revived *jus-primus-noctus* upon my old bones.

The dress gleamed in the closet like a shroud, or the cassock of a goddess, flanged whimsically at the hem and the shoulders. Although I then had a thirty-four waist and Lily a twenty-four, her shoulders are well-developed from competitive swimming and her hips I have described before. I quite easily slipped the gown down the length of my body—even managing to fasten many of the tiny pearl buttons into their questioning loops—sufficiently to walk around the darkened living room and out to the terrace, the laugher of my girls fading into whispered speculations & asides, the confidences of two young women who had taken to each other like twins.

As I stepped back into our room from the terrace, still hearing the high, sweet voices of *les girls,* I saw my father standing at the door. Tall, spectral in a loose-limbed dressing gown from *Sulka,* in Paris, his eyes looked past me—failed to find me—and gradually returned to Lily's gown as if it were a lighthouse beaming at ships struggling in the sea. He appeared as a ghost, like Hamlet's father, except for the visible command he held over the scene. And he spoke: "I see you have taken a turn from your wedding which if you do not leave it on the floor this instant will make you both unhappy—: leave it now, as newly-weds; wait for your middle age, as I did, before experimenting along these lines. You'll find yourself adopting *a slower method."*

"This was after mother died, I presume, when you yearned to honor your *feminine side?"* I answered. "Or did she dress up in your suits as if to go off to the law courts of Boston?"

"Not at all—as to the latter: As you must know, men's clothes have increasingly crept into women's fashion over the years, and there is little need to portray themselves as men though many of them may have strong masculine sides. As we reached fifty, I discovered Lily's father, a new law school graduate, and your dear mother found comfort and passion in another woman, a dazzling professor of mathematics at Wellesley—of all places!"

A wan, puzzled, sleep-worn Rafael appeared in the doorway behind my father just as the girls' voices stopped their song, as crickets do when you come upon them in the night and clap your hands. The encounter with my father could not continue as I now heard Lily come into the bathroom and turn on the water in the whirlpool. I heard Diana's laughter above the stream and even smelled the infusion of bath oils. My women of Greece! My father turned and offered a salute behind his head as he left the room. I withdrew to the terrace and sank into a deep yellow canvas chair to listen to the loitering bars of the orchestra on the yacht below. The wind blew in time with halyards.

I had not noticed the abrupt stillness in my daughter's room, or the sound of the door locked in the bathroom between our two rooms, which also shared a small sitting room, this *petit-salon* —a feature much appreciated by friends at Fairchild School, just outside Boston, I'd invited down for winter holidays—closed off from the living room by a separate entrance. I flung myself into the long, narrow walk-in closet and extracted myself from the wedding dress at the moment Lily came into our room, laughing.

"I'm just putting your dress away," I called. "Would you like to bathe together?" I wanted to wash away father's recent image. "No love—Diana and I are getting into the whirlpool for a bit, just half an hour. Can you wait for me as long as that...*eternity?*"

"In our life together, I'll do the waiting while you do the catching-up. As you've said, we've already met at thirty, midway, and the future will be a sequence of plateaus where we meet again and again in the middle of our ages, and even when you're sixty and I'm eighty, we'll both be seventy—"

"Dad, *leave it!*" Diana teased as she came into the room in my white terry robe. "I've been hearing what a good *teacher* you are, so don't spoil it. Just act your age, which Lily loves, and then she'll act hers and become mother of my step-siblings!" Diana was to start college in the Fall, also at Amherst, so I saw that I would have her shadowing the same hallways—or similar ones—as Lily for the next two years, reminding me what kind of husband I should be now that she had out-grown the need of my fathering.

The *sisters-in-law* retreated into the bathroom, where the giant tub was filling and steaming and about to circulate its florid waters in a far more forbearing *Charybdis* at whose center I was to be submerged in my own hubris and arise suitably prepared for marriage of a very young woman to a forty-year-old man-child.

I left the sliding glass doors all night open to the Intercoastal Waterway, as the sheltered draperies were now blowing into the room like a sail: and back towards the terrace like a boat tacking; now and then they ballooned into a great, soaring spinnaker which filled half the bedroom. The girls stayed a long time in the whirlpool, and I fell asleep to their splashing and the throbbing of the jets. I awakened thinking we were sailing out across Buzzards Bay, out to Falmouth, on the Cape, and perhaps even to Martha's Vineyard—a stretch for a day-sail, moored overnight, perhaps in Cuttyhunk.

Lily had left a note beneath a glass of orange juice saying she was playing tennis with Diana at the Everglades Club, and it seemed very early as my father had not appeared with promised coffee and croissants—actually, he had not so served us since the morning we were married. As I wandered to the kitchen to make coffee I could sense the house was empty and, glancing into the master bedroom suite, and then into Rafael's room—both joined similarly to mine and Diana's by a bathroom, making a symmetry surrounding the great room, and dining area—I could see they had gone out, though it was just after seven. As it was Sunday, I knew they had both left for the farmers' market in West Palm. I sat at my father's desk, a long 'refectory' table from some monastery in Europe, and began to sketch my plans for the future before Lily and me in California and Massachusetts. It was early to reach my contacts in Los Angeles, so I thought I'd try calling Amherst to see about shifting teaching semesters around so we could spend the winter in Los Angeles, and then, at noon, I'd call my former agent out there who'd come to the wedding and ask about work. I was surprised how easily everything fell into place at her feet

Lily left me five years later to live with Diana. Together they raised our son, Jocyln, named after his great uncle Fairchild. The christening had been at a Quaker meetinghouse in on Horse Neck Road in South Dartmouth where we all live on exemplary terms within a mile of each other. I have accepted their union equably, and sometimes wonder if Lily had been searching for her lost twin, the first Lily, and found her in Diana—not as a mere lover, but as someone, who, when she touched her, felt like she was touching herself—feeling whole again. If so, I may have a same need, nearing fifty, living with my own twin sister Leah in our grandmother's farm house with now only eighty acres for sheep and hay. I also kept Lily's wedding dress, no longer to wear it myself, but offered it to Lee to celebrate our union following her twenty-year marriage to a French painter, André Vuillard.

Leah's—Lee we call her—son André, after his father, is now in Boston managing the Gallery in Newbury Street which Lee started over twenty-five years ago when she graduated from Radcliffe with an MFA in fine Arts. He, and my daughter, appear to have accepted our living arrangements—"it's not as if you could have children," he scowled—and as our nuptials were held outside Massachusetts where no one knew us, we returned as Mr. & Mrs. Fairchild. We continued celebrating the anniversary of the loss of our parents in 1956, when we both were ten, in the sinking of the *Andrea Doria* off Nantucket. For the past five years, after Lily left me, Lee and I have made the pilgrimage to Nantucket and swum out in the ocean to embrace their souls in the tides.

Every morning, when Lee and I awake, coiled in our sheets, she makes me tea and brings scones made from whatever grows on the farm or along the river: rose hips, from September's beach roses; concord grapes from vines tangling with bull brier and honeysuckle and sly sumac; and even the last cranberries not yet harvested from the bogs and fens very close to us. We preserve much of these fruits, and spill them into our daily lives during the winter, embracing all the other rituals, which consecrate our life together and make it certain. Our father died down in Palm Beach a few years after the wedding: his service was held at Bethesda-by-the-Sea. He never returned to Boston, as far as we could determine, and spent his last months with Lily's father in his villa on the Inter Coastal Waterway, a passage which seemed never to begin, and never to end— and it reminded me of another waterway: the Cape Cod Canal, rushing its currents back and forth amid great oil tankers and other ships, its ancient railroad bridge rising and lowering to admit only the bravest seafarers.

Lily made me think of that, and Lee made me want to live it: a life of bravery and resolve, simple and chaste in its elements, yet passionate in its moments—though we had only a small boat and a narrow bed to share our dreams in—which sustained us without doubt. If Lily fell in love with her twin, and then with Diana, I could only accept my twin as an all-nurturing bride—who else was there, with all the Fairchilds gone and we the remaining signposts—and who was left to guide us over thresholds which no longer existed? I came to understand life repeating itself in fine-spun circles; each offered protection for the next step, or wish or oracular gesture towards immortality–if such might await me.

At Thanksgiving last year, everyone came to our house—: Lily and Diana; Joclyn, now ten and lunging into his future; Lee's son André, and his girlfriend who helps with the gallery; and the pastor of our Friends meeting. Lily came beside me and took my hand to her lips. "Life has turned out perfectly for all of us: I still love you, and love Diana. Our child loves us both and—you and Lee are finally, fully together. Ours lives are matched, tied, bound forever."

I gave myself plenty of time to envision her remark as I walked days later around the 200 acre farm I had bought for my *wife* Lily, but deeded to Allen's Pond Sanctuary of the Massachusetts Audubon Society as a preserve, she retaining a life tenancy. It had been owned by an old Portuguese farmer with no heirs whose family had come to New Bedford from the Azores in 1880 for whaling. In the barn I sat in an abandoned buggy, its seat sagging and its wheels broken and reins long withered to blackened strips. Light came in through small panes and parted a perpetual dust to reveal an ancient tractor and bailer, long ago superannuated from the fields, and pieces of discarded furniture, it seemed, huddling against a brace of stones supporting a sidewall.

Here Lily came to me on light steps of contrition and wide eyes of love. "You've done wonders with the place," I laughed.

"We've really done nothing, except in the house, of course. I so wanted this to be a working farm again, sheep for shearing, and hay for stacking—Diana spends her time up at the gallery—"

"—so she's up in Boston with Lee and André—?" I whispered against a soft mood pondering its place in our lives as she stepped bravely towards me.

"Oh—*I've missed you!* I want my man, and his son wants his father. Don't you know, you old goat, whose every whisker and wrinkle I've longed for? Our experiments in living are about to end! Diana wants Lee's son André, and Lee—*will give you up!*"

"Give me up?" Good lord child, *we live together as a couple!*"

"She can't tell you— she wants to marry a Tufts professor—"

"Then she can take you with her as a *châtelaine au maison!*"

"As a housekeeper, I'd scrub floors to be yours!" she flashed.

"Not something you'd have considered five years ago—?"

"I was a child—can you ever forgive me for that?" she wept, and pulled on my coat sleeves.

"Forgive you for seducing Diana? You must be joking—!" I knew, then, I had no further ground.

"What about my wedding dress?" she began to wail. "It belongs to me—no matter who else has worn it—" she cried as she crept closer to me with no hesitation as she out her arms around my waist.

"Give it to your *twin*, Diana—let's keep it in the family!"

"If I wore it, would you marry me again?" she pleaded.

Her voice faded into a darkened corner I had never met before: she was defiant—grown into a woman I had not been allowed to know. If, a chrysalis had turned from a pupa into assured flight, I had no measure of its glory. I stared at her without sanction or forgiveness. "Ask again."

"If I wore this dress, would you marry me again?"

"I thought you'd never ask," I laughed, just fast enough to catch her leaping into my arms, as wide an embrace as dreamed.

—from *Saw Grass Trilogy*, 2002: Palm Beach Florida

Blaine & Blaine

At sixteen I had two loves, both named Blaine, who dwelled diurnally in my heart you might say, living in different time zones so I enjoyed them more in daylight—like a time-traveler, my physics teacher may have said—than perhaps I deserved, my New England Quaker patrimony would have thought. One was a boy, my roommate at a fine venerable Massachusetts preparatory school; the other a girl, a second cousin in Utah, where my mother's family have been, like my father's in Boston, for over a century-and-a-half. Her flying red hair and fast riding hid shyness which masked a passion I came to find.

She, Blaine, a year older, and I had fallen in love the summer before, where we both worked on my grandfather's ranch with many of his other teenage grandchildren. The girls cooked and the boys drove cattle across ten thousand acres and bucked a thousand bales of hay daily. She took me to bed in the stables just a week before I returned east to become Blaine Saltonstall's roommate, grandson of governor Leverett. My few nights with *Blainey*—as everyone but I called her—were like a cantabile: I took away a memory of her singing amid the gentle, curious snorting and stamping of the horses, and the percussive crackle of the hay beneath us. We pledged going to college together and marrying.

Blaine clasped my arms in an easy, fraternal greeting the first day of school. He leaned back in a gracious swagger to assess me. "My, you've filled out this summer—all that healthy western life, I'd guess—and you brought your cowboy boots, I see, but I doubt Headmaster will let you wear them to classes! May I try them on?"

"Sure—but they won't fit your—"

"—my right leg, you were going say?" he laughed, brightly forgiving.

For Blaine was taken with polio as a child, in the 'fifties, and his right foot was as a child's, half the size of his left; his right calf had been wizened to the size of his wrist, but his thigh was massive and powerful. Although he ran, even hopped with a limp, he played all the fast sports—soccer, tennis and track. *Blainey's* legs were long and sinuous, full in their curves, and also powerful from riding her pinto quarter horse mix in barrel races at the rodeo. I tried the bucking broncs, but never got eight seconds. Calf-roping and bull-dogging was barely my tempo. She left me at the Salt Lake airport Labor Day weekend, both of us heart-sore.

Private schools start the year no earlier than a week after, and so I had ten days to long for Blainey yet feel the rousing charge through my veins of seeing my fellows and pick up mythologies we had left behind in June. Blaine had not the year before been a close pal, but we had been JV teammates together and I had felt the pull of his unbounded courage and enthusiasm. We were awkward the first night in our room together, like newlyweds, until he came over to my bed and slipped his hand under the cover. "We may as well sort this out right away, until we see some girls!"

I haven't seen Blaine since college, where he and I and Blainey were all together. When my uncle Joclyn, 'Jock' Fairchild believed that I was set on marrying my Utah cousin and as she and I had both been admitted to Brown— not the Harvard of three generations of Fairchilds—he pledged to pay, from my late father's estate, all expenses and an allowance to us. We were married as freshmen and lived on the top floor of an old bow-fronted house on Wickenden Street; Blaine lived with an aunt in a fine brick Federal house up Benefit Street, across from RISD where he had decided to study Design. I pursued engineering for the family business.

At graduation, I was off to M.I.T. but both Blaines held back a few weeks in Providence, to continue in a summer curriculum, and Blainey gave up our Wickenden apartment to move into Blaine's aunt's house.

"It's only for the summer," she pleaded, "and I need to finish the work in painting I neglected. I'll be in Cambridge in no time—*our time!*"

'Our time' lengthened into *their time* and took them to Oxford's Ruskin School of Drawing and Fine Art where Blainey, still married to me, had a daughter. Blaine was in the London branch of his family's bank. We were estranged, if not divorced,

I now face after fifty years a reunion at our preparatory school, where we shall be accorded great honors as the 'Admirals'—a private cruise on the school's legendary schooner; exclusive dinners with the Headmaster as we, in our late 'sixties, are wooed to figure the school in our estate planning: life bequests before the grave. After uncle Jock died I took Fairchild Electronics from its prominence on Route 128 to a peninsula south of San Francisco, where companies called 'Intel' and 'HP' were starting up with great ferocity. Selling our family firm—which had been given birth in 1957 after sale of the old Fairchild textile mills—three times, each event diluting previous stockholders *except* Fairchilds, I figured we were richer than Blaine's family, notwithstanding the heroic efforts of State Street Bank over the generations. The question suddenly became, when Blaine and I face off at the reunion, would we ponder any *rapprochement* between his wife, *my* Blainey, and me, or just match our two checkbooks for the greater gift to the school, and might parade our successes beneath the banner of the Academy. In my dim, primitive expectations I could only think of *who won Blainey,* not even who had excelled on the far-ago playing fields, or scored highest academic feats—never to play upon their later lives—; but I learned, through the current class secretary, that Blaine's life was much diminished through financial reverses that often occur when the idle rich take investments into their own hands, and that his wife Blainey suffered at sixty-nine from obscure ailments not specified: When I faced them, she might be in a wheel chair.

"What are you worrying about?" my daughter Fiona demanded as I rehearsed these premonitions before her and her husband. "It's March, the reunion is June! These people left your life before you knew yourself! Just show up and enjoy the spectacle—we're coming too!" Fiona had been admitted in the early years of girls attending the all-male academy.

Southeast winds were blowing across Buzzard's Bay from Falmouth and the ocean beyond the Cape. Halyards rang a chaste *chorale* across the harbor, as a rare out-going tide pulled the boats' moorings around to lee. The school was covered in a drowsy canopy of fog, lighted above by a bright aura from the moon and other celestial lights hanging above the storm like pendants watching and waiting over the sea. I stood on a stone pier in front of the main commons building, where numerous small launches and large dories were tied down to ferry passengers out to larger sea-going vessels.

I had arrived early to survey the campus, now elongated a near half-mile along the main road past new classrooms, art studios and an applied science center which I had helped to create with gifts over the years I had been absent, save for scant reunions and the graduation of our daughter Fiona. I was the first there and restless without foreboding: I was waiting for the appearance of the one classmate who would make a reunion satisfying, Blaine Saltonstall, tethered to his wife, *my* Blaine...

The sun crowned the taut weather vane on the top of the main building, just as the naval clock sounded eight bells from its belfry aloft. I searched the arrival grounds for signs of headlights probing the field for places to park around the goalposts, looking spectral instead of sentinel. I watched a massive white tent being pulled up where hundreds would sit for meals and stand with drinks and dance—except for our class, which would dine with the headmaster. 'Admirals' were to be suitably housed.

Fiona will be coming too. Unknown to Blaine and me, we had made a baby shortly before graduation from Brown. Fiona had been born at Oxford, after Blaine and Blaine went off together. Now she is forty-five, and her son—my grandson—graduated on the same playing field where I am standing. Both Blaines insisted Fiona take my name, Fairchild, and assured me she was mine: they did not sleep together until at Oxford. My girl teaches at Brown and her *e-mail, fionafair@Brown.edu,* gives me a leap of wonder and thankfulness whenever I see it. Her mother and I have never let go our bonds of cousinage, and through our letters and hidden visits we have become as dear to each other as we were so long ago. We both live in Back Bay, I in my grandmother's house on Charles Street, she nearby. I never married again, but for thirty years kept a beloved French-woman, Thérèse, a chatelaine you might say, of my father's gallery and apartment on Rue de Seine until his death. Our two children live in France and I've long keep the *pied à terre* in Rue de Seine.

Fiona's drive down to Marion from Providence is the same as mine from Boston, so she will be coming soon. I had offered to bring Blaine and Blainey in my car, but as she is ill and travels with a nurse they prefer their own transport. We have adjoining rooms, and Fiona will stay with her mother and Blaine will bunk with me for the weekend, but they will be late. I am resting against a giant sea anchor embedded in granite as I begin to weep bitterly as the wind shifts to a kinder southwest face from Northeast.

"Solomon! What a wonderful poem you posted in the galley of the schooner this morning—and here you are at last with Blaine, our all-New England-cup-holder in three sports!" Headmaster raised a glass to read:

> ### All-a-Taut-o
> Hear the eight delicate bells of midnight
> Sounding the commander's watchful zeal;
> The shallow hills of Falmouth shed their
> light,
> Gray smiles across a starboard reach: ideal
> Union of wind and tide, love's surety
> Leans the blissful hull into nourishment;
> Mizzen and main point with alacrity
> As fore jib snaps in surprised bereavement.
> Eight bells again, now harsh in midday lee;
> The faintly scented decks pillow our
> stance,
> Braced then climbing the unknown
> odyssey,
> Elegy of unexpected dreams—chance:
>
> The life we thought we had prepared to
> find
> Has overspread the weather helm of mind.
>
> (Under sail, Buzzards Bay)

Sonnet: June, 2014 S.F.

Added Couplets: The Voyage Home

Top gallants no more sear the horizon,
The Coast Guard said, "canvas much too brazen!"
For those in peril on the sea,
whose fathers served in a Dutch Navy;
or those who still their canvas keep—
Sou'sou-east of Orion's feet:
I introduce the compass of my soul—:
A hundred foot schooner with iron hull.

—Solomon MacCleod Fairchild

"I'm sure the toasts are more for Blaine than me," I told my Blainey.

"Nonsense! You two were equal heroes in my mind—and that's a lot of years to remember, don't you agree, Blaine?" We both looked intently, not sure whom she had addressed—Saltonstall or Fairchild—but Fiona, sitting on the other side of her mother, eased the quandary into calmer waters. "Yes, they were champions to so many of us here tonight!" Blaine had come across the parade ground in a wheel chair, but she had walked with a cane up to the Head-of-School's residence. Her husband Blaine fell into a stupor after the drinks beneath the great, flying spinnaker of a tent and had nodded off during dinner, only to revive himself, as a governor's grandson, and proclaim his love for and loyalty to the school, even opening a checkbook at the table, which Blainey snatched back into her lap.

"What happened to him?" I whispered to my beloved. "Who is he I loved so much on this very campus? You never told me about your lives!"

I felt Fiona's hand on mine, gently remanding it to my lap. "You'll have plenty of time this weekend to look for those answers, if you really want them, *pater"* — our intimacy had led us into Latin declamations—"I am convinced." I could only ask the fugitive couple about their children.

"Wonderfully!" Blaine woke to the question—and I then recalled his frequent answering my questions with his own in those boyhood days—: he had a faster, superior footing than I, and always smirked at me shyly when he had raced ahead, but always circled back to find me, to bring me into his orbit. "Our son, John—ha! we have enough *Blaines*—is in the Navy, Captain in the Pacific. Gerald, alas, went into Harvard Divinity—"

"—how wonderful!" Fiona rushed in. "Will he...'take orders' in a church, if that's the term, or would he teach in a seminary—?"

"Damned if I know—he could become one of those *mesmerists*, from the nineteenth century; he has those fancies, like Mary Baker Eddy—"

"*Leave it,* Blaine," his wife called softly from her chair.

"Yes, Blainey." He bowed his head to her as a supplicant at the vestry.

As I heard this simple, plaintive exchange of their names—*my names*—I fell in love with them again as if I had been across a continent, a lasting diurnal affection, and saw again how she, in college, had shared us like twins and I, poor fool, had shared her with Blaine—divided my love for each of them until they found their own. I stood up and held my chair.

"Dad?" Fiona took my hand. I stumbled to one knee, caught myself.

"I need to walk outside," I gasped. Headmaster stared hard at me, his face blanched with remorse.

"It's all right, my dear," Blainey laughed as she too rose on her cane.

"Are we all invalids here?" I cried as I turned towards the door, seeking release from an ill-defined lament pulling upon my memory.

"Not at all in the sense you fear, dear Solomon-of-the-ages. You and Blaine will share a room this weekend, and I know it will become clear—you may discover a belated...*jus primus noctus* while I drowse in a life of a daughter's love. Farewell, my princes. May your dreams forgive you—"

What I remember of the night, and the nights after, is of no concern. Very late, Blaine and I were stumbling along the school's great floating wharf, rising and falling in the turn of the tide, and we sat numbly on the small beach listening to six bells, *ding-ding, ding-ding, ding-ding* at three?

We all appeared at eight bells—was it 7:30 and were we navigating to breakfast by *dead reckoning?*—ready to board a launch out to the schooner in the middle of the harbor. Our spirits were high—Blaine and I still riding on a crest of early morning Guinness from a cooler in his car—and Blainey striding along the dock without her cane, just arm-in-arm in Fiona's careful foot-falls along the dock, the sun high and the wind strong from the North. "We'll go out to Falmouth on a broad reach, and round Cuttyhunk when the wind shifts!" Blaine promised us because *he knew.*

"Darling, you haven't sailed in twenty years," my Blaine laughed. I saw them together, Blaine & Blaine, like the name of a shipwright, fast in its sinecure along an ancient coast; or a chandler provisioning a Flying Dutchman lost at sea. I called out that Blaine and I would sail again soon.

The ship, built in 1914, is now one hundred years along, and as we stood on deck, unseen computers—undreamed of in 1964—pulled up the mizzen, then the main as they directed the refitted engines to take us out of the harbor and finally allow the jibs to point with alacrity. "It wasn't like this in our day, was it Solly? We hauled the lines and sheets around a stubborn winch at best." I choked back an answer hearing his old nickname for me: hearing 'Solomon' an unsettling "mystery." He was right: the faculty and students took it up in a bright choral tribute I never heard again. Below decks, where I had seated my Blaine in the trim salon, she kissed me and sang in a clear and liquid canticle, "All is well—and I pray you have never doubted that—*my first love.*"

Orient Point

As I sat on the narrow dock in New London—confounded by the train from home, Boston's Back Bay, disappearing behind me, and the fugitive sense of leaving my boarding school classmates on the South Coast of Massachusetts—I shrank in the loneliness of my great black trunk beside me, packed with my clothes for a summer away from home. The Ferry, due to embark in an hour, would arrive at Orient Point, at the tip of the North Fork of Long Island, where I hoped to be met by my father's close friends from East Hampton, on the South Fork, and their daughter Grace, with whom I'd been in love since I was thirteen—she a radiant fifteen.

I was sixteen, and Grace was eighteen, bound for Wellesley in the fall. Now I am sixty-six, so this *recherché*, if it's that, is a half century past but as vivid as the moment I saw her in a floral, smocked dress from Liberty's flying from the open sunroof of her mother's Jaguar. Her kisses fled across to the arriving ferry, even as taut sailors gathered the lines around balding cleats in the narrow harbor. Her mother Millicent, also my *guardian*, watched from the car as I dragged my inhospitable trunk from the ferry and Grace raced across the dock to kiss me, tossing her flaming russet hair around my face and allowing me to cup her small, hidden breasts in a secret we had given ourselves at past holidays. She promised she would wait for me two years before we made love in bed: she had not. We fell into love naturally.

I had been in boys' boarding schools since I was ten, in 1956, when my mother was lost in the sinking of *Andrea Doria* off Nantucket. My father travelled constantly so his brother, my uncle Jocelyn—a long-settled bachelor in Boston's Back Bay—sheltered my twin sister and me in extravagant home schooling. This past Spring, not having been with Grace since Christmas when we skied and fell like snow angels kissing each other's whitened eyelids, I had tried to bear her absence by taking a lover from my class and the JV lacrosse team—we both turned sixteen in April, the same month of Grace's 18th when I sent so many flowers, the bursar at school had to call Uncle Jocelyn to cover my account, which had been extravagantly funded by grieving family to allow me to take friends on sailing picnics—regattas, really, as far as Falmouth and Woods Hole at the end of Buzzards Bay—and to plays up in Boston, with suppers in Scully Square afterwards always chaperoned by young sympathetic teachers and their dates or faculty wives.

"Cutie-kins! Fuzzie-wuzie!" Grace cried out as she stroked my nascent beard, whispered behind my ear, "it's for keeps." She offered a life-long pledge...

Her mother, full of fun and hi-jinks herself, watched us indulgently from the Jaguar. She had appointed herself my 'guardian mother' although my father, in absentia with a new wife, remained *jus primus sanguinis* as far as

Commonwealth law provided, with Uncle Jocelyn his successor. Her husband, a lawyer in New York City holding a seat in the State Assembly, was from an old Dutch line on Long Island, Piet Vandermeer. Millicent, a member of a faded British aristocracy with no prospects for the end of the Second War and many enemies because of her father's fascist sympathies, came to New York in 1940 with little more than her passage, two trunks filled with Chanel gowns, traced with Eddie Duchin, and jewelry, which had come to her at the end of the First War. She discovered Piet, just out of Yale Law School, at a society tea dance. Their first daughter, Philomena, was born in 1942; Grace in 1944; *and I*—the outlier—in 1946; four years later my mother died.

Yes, I had sprouted a low crop of blonde hair across my face since Christmas and began to shave, first with a brush and lather like my father then with an exotic, almost fugitive electric razor which Santi brought to school after Easter break. I could see Millicent giggling by her car as her daughter rubbed her face against my fur and drew her tongue across an ear hidden from her mother's view from the dockyard. "You may be a minor still and me just barely and adult, but *you're mine!* I told mom about my waiting for you in college, and dad became purple in his stogy way, but they're ok. We'll spend the summer playing tennis and sailing and behaving ourselves—until that beard grows in: *I'll be defenseless!*"

"Dear-Heart, our very own *Solomon-of-the-ages!*" Millicent trumpeted as she strode towards us in Christian Science virtue—for that was her faith, a penitent of Mary

Baker Eddy—'that old fortune-teller from Back Bay' our uncle Jocelyn and before him grandfather Seth Fairchild used to say. We had been Quakers for over two centuries and liked to wear our spiritual gowns loosely. Millicent discovered the faith as her husband struggled through his abstemious Presbyterian dogma to ordain, establish a patrician practice—she reeled him in like a sodden carp—and the religion overran him. But not his daughters: the elder, Philomena, fled to Catholic certitude; Grace drifted in my direction to The Society of Friends. Millicent's frivolity, disguising its sibilant undertones, drew the young swain towards her, as her daughter pulled aside to a dryer shore. I was trapped in an enormous *fête champêtre* as her mother led us into a *valse caprice* of wide-gathered distractions at her club where I would be entertained as a juvenile, and fear Grace would turn toward other suitors. It did not happen: She came to me—and, it came to be, never let go. "Letting go is not giving up," she proclaimed.

As we drove along the North Fork to meet another ferry to Sag Harbor, Grace sat beside me in the back of the Jag where we folded down the walnut desks to compare our school work, scribbling away at fevered manifestos and obscure equations, holding hands beneath our pens until I slipped an emerald and diamond ring of my mother's onto Grace's hand, indisputably my right to give her, and her duty to accept. She threw the hand over the broad leather back of the seat to her mother, who slowed the car to accept the fancy of her daughter and the unseen, outstretched hand of the Fairchilds of Boston in the supine summer of 1962, covering us with dazzling cerulean skies.

Summer with her came and went, an ebb and flow of tides not solely devoted to sailing, as we had expected, but the more constrained rigors of a couple in danger, to be supervised and channeled in their courtship. We found time alone, and held ourselves to our pledge of chastity and fidelity until we were to be married in two years. Accordingly, we often slept together, kissed and touched each other liberally, but kept to our vows. She wore my mother's magnificent ring everywhere, and her parents did not object, thinking perhaps it was a twenty thousand dollar friendship ring! Millicent called us 'lovebirds' yet kept a close watch, wrapped up in her confusion of how to offer her daughter to the world: as a senior in college married to a sophomore—an admired youth from a prominent and rich Boston family—; or as a girl who truly bloomed on the arm of an older man, established in his profession, as Piet had found her long ago.

At summer's last days, fading over Georgica Pond, Grace and I were permitted to take the ferry back to New England, with her belongings safely packed in Millicent's Jag, on board, to carry her to Wellesley and me to my uncle Jocelyn in Charles Street, to be returned to eleventh grade. I can't take from my vision the narrowing spit of low, pine-swept land at Orient Point, vanishing abruptly into the Sound. Scrub pine and spartina grasses leaned into the wind, and I wept on the upper deck not knowing if I was leaving my life behind, or sailing by dead reckoning in into an unknown *wine dark sea:* I loved our future life more than mine.

"Everything is as it should be my darling boy," Grace assured me. "I await you, by this ring: You taught me to sail, and to become a bride—and I became your bride!"

I was fortunate, I supposed, that Grace was in a woman's college a safe ten or twelve miles west of Harvard and Tufts, and I was locked safely away in a boy's prep school. We wrote weekly, and when she could spare a weekend from her avid study of art history and playing field hockey, she came to stay with me at my uncle's and ailing grandmother's house.

"So many of the girls start dreaming of the day they will find husbands, as if Wellesley is a breeding ground for *fated* unions!" she said as we walked huddled against snow blowing across the Common. "I already know my husband, and believe I'll go to graduate school." It was Twelfth Night of my senior year, January 6th, and my eighteenth birthday. We were trudging over to a carillon service at an Episcopal church on Boylston where Nativity songs would be sung by *We Three Kings*. I had been accepted not at Harvard, where my father and grandfather had gone, but at Brown, in Providence, a mere thirty minutes from Wellesley.

"When we marry," she mused, her head tucked away in my muffler, "are we to live in Providence or Boston? As you finish your first year and I my third, I can easily transfer down to RISD—where I'd love to study painting—or we could stay up here, and you could go to M.I.T., where your family's company beckons you." I protested joining Fairchild Electronics, yet it was fated.

"Darling, you love science," she continued. Your uncle Jocelyn has no heirs and you no siblings except your sister who will open a gallery."

"Of course you're right. And my father will never come back from Paris, where he is reliving his last days with my mother—"

"—*so*, we'll marry in June, and live together in Providence or at Cambridge!" she cried as we rushed up the church steps. "All's well, pet."

As we walked back from the church to Charles Street, the snow had stopped and the moon hung like a pendant dropping through the fog in a frail blue reflection of Grace in her lapis-lazuli earrings and necklace. I took her arm for the first time like a man fully established in manhood. She surrendered her face to my shoulder, and kissed my ear in a cloak of her hair, which concealed the path ahead. "*Yes, now,*" she whispered. I had only to turn the key in my grandmother's house and Grace followed, then drew me to my room. We opened the window, where the night air was warm after the snow, and gave us a soft, forgiving breeze, even warming us until we removed our clothes and shivered with discovery of our bodies. We kissed and touched as we had not attempted the summer before, and could not let go of ourselves until she excused herself to my bathroom: "You may as well know, I'm prepared. I have a diaphragm, unused, of course—we'll wait some years for children—It's 1964, love, and such things are easily come by." I watched her arched back and long, taut legs disappear only to return as a woman grown beyond my grasp—until she offered our union, far from worried about blood on the sheets, and pulled me into the center of my life, far from that shoal at Orient Point which left me so desolate. We slept briefly, then searched for each other again as equals; she was astride me as an equine conquest and she whispered *this is for keeps*— falling forward crying—*until June!*

"I think you'll find this apartment very suitable for you and your wife," a small man of kindness and probity showed us an apartment adjacent to the Brown campus at the upper end of Wickenden Street. "Very short walk to the School of Design, just along Benefit Street. As you're both in school and so young, you won't mind the climb to the top floor—which, as you see, has a deep bay window across the front of the house. And, it's the largest unit."

Grace and I looked up at the old house, hewn of grey granite with a broad and suddenly pinched face like a battleship from Pearl Harbor in 1941—a point of great sensitivity to Rhode Islanders, who lost so many sailors that December 7th and still celebrated the country's only V-J Day, a reference our landlord was unlikely to entertain. "The whole top floor, *twelve-hundred square feet!* The other floors have been divided in *two* flats," he added, "and I live on the ground floor, front, to assist you—"

"Yes, Mr. Slocum, it's all wonderful!" Grace exclaimed. "So much light, facing south. And as we're not likely to have children for several years, the stairs will keep us fit—don't you see, dear-heart, it's perfect? And with *two* bedrooms, both our sisters can visit, even *together*, unmarried."

This was awkward, as Philomena was in a convent and my twin sister, at Radcliffe, was a declared lesbian—until she met her French husband, a painter—André Vuillard—who washed up on Newbury Street. *Vuillard's great grandson!*

"I have your uncle's letter, Mr. Fairchild, guaranteeing full rent and utilities until you graduate—1968 is it?—or you may transfer to another university. Where or when could that be—?" he pressed a kindly, avuncular meaning.

"My wife will graduate here in two years, Mr. Slocum. At that point, I have agreed to return to Boston and enter M.I.T. to prepare myself for the family business." Grace stood by patiently as I recited this *entente-cordiale*, hoping I would one day take her to Paris and my father's realm.

"We'll," he concluded, you will settle in August? Here are two sets of the keys. I keep a third—just in case." Mr. Slocum's patrimony, well established, was gratifying to have beneath our first roof.

My father's 'realm' in Paris consisted of a suite of rooms atop a *belle-époque* hotel in Rue de Seine, which he shared with a decathlon mistress Thérèse, who he had met after my mother died. On the ground floor he owned a gallery where he showed unknown French painters and sent them on to Boston to be introduced by my sister, who also owned a gallery. I cabled him, as I turned nineteen and Grace twenty-one, an invitation to our wedding at the Longfellow Friends meeting house in Cambridge, June 10th, 1965. He replied: DELIGHTED TO HEAR OF YOUR NUPTIALS STOP. SHALL STAY AT RITZ WITH THéRèSE & CHILDREN—NO PLACE FOR THEM AT CHéZ MAMAM— HOPE TO GO DOWN TO SOUTHCOAST FARM—CAN I HOST AN EVENT THERE OR BOSTON? JOCLYN OPAQUE, COMME D'HABITUDE BUT I AM WITH YOU & GRACE WITH BLAZING CHEVRONS. *PATER ETERNIS.* Not having seen him in ten years, I blushed, not knowing his last days with mother aboard *Andrea Doria*, July, 1956.

"So that's my father-in-law!" Grace laughed. "You've been blessed! And a sister with a gallery on Newbury Street," she added with extraneous pride.

"Whatever can you mean? Have I just missed something in those lines?"

"He's telling you to look between the lines—a telegram is, you see, much like a poem: full of compression, and always *about itself*—"

"So I have only to look between the lines to capture ten years? I should have taken you to Paris to meet him—that would have been a....pre-nuptial fête-champêtre!"

"Yes! He loves you, and knew uncle Jock would care for you. Paris was the place he could grieve for your mother, and find another woman!"

"It sounds rather like one of those inflamed plays my grandmother, upstairs, used to love, fifty years ago, to ornament the stage with relief."

"Will you ever relent, my darling *husband*, and accept what's near?"

Grace's parents came ambivalently to the wedding from

Long Island, encouraged because they could combine a trip to Marblehead to prowl for antiques, which had become Millicent's life since she surrendered the salvation of two daughters. Philomena attended, with fellow novitiates, and my sister appeared in slacks and a blazer emblazoned, *Radcliffe Redux!* with a girl on her arm dressed as from a brigade of suffragettes. My father welcomed Grace to the Fairchild fold so exuberantly she wept. The pastor spoke sparingly, offering a *Quakerly* assurance our youth would rise into the light, and find abundance always, not scarcity. The reception was lavish, but we early escaped back to Wickenden Street.

"How far we've come, in two years and a half—need I count the miracles since we resolved at Orient Point to mate?—: We have so far to go, and all the time to get there, if there is a *there!* You've done it, *made me safe!*"

I questioned her sweet dependency as a road leading her to a strong, independent woman like my mother, and determined to unmask her childhood which I understood more that my own. We made gifts to each other each day—sometimes remembrance of a favorite blend of tea; other-times, more grave assessments of her studies and mine, fine arts & science, blended into a conclave of higher learning and a fervent path to sharing knowledge that took us back to pasta with mussels and white wine and bed—always bed—where whatever diverged between us during the day, converged, and made us more than the sum of our two selves—I *cherished* her, and that kept our teapot brimming with its embroidered cozy from my grandmother; Grace acceded to my impudence as I teased her about the *blots & blurs* of impressionism, and she scaled my hide about gravity bending light to its own uses, just as her light fell upon me with no assistance from the heavens. As she read to me about Roger Fry and Virginia Wolfe, I offered my notes on integrated circuitry and semi-conductors which, Uncle Joclyn promised us, would make us all much richer than the shabby mill-owners we had long been.

When she graduated, Grace set her sights on the Ruskin School of Fine Arts at Oxford; Uncle Jocelyn relented, and sent me along to attend Merton College in engineering for two years. We made our home in England, and our twin daughters, Fiona and Penelope, were born within its tender carapace—enchantment we held dearly.

We loved cycling around Oxford's sacred lanes, and especially up the towpath along the Thames with a twin riding in a 'snuggly' strapped to each of our backs. From an early age, the girls loved to look ahead to where we were going, and as they neared two, pull our ears to indicate which way to turn—usually toward the browsing cows—and look at each other and squeal in their soaring alpine postures. Grace and I took them everywhere—to the Bodleian for concerts and readings; evening Shakespeare in college gardens, from *Lear* to *As You Like it,* where they slept on a blanket while we had cakes & ale and Grace wept at heroines such as Rosalind disguised themselves as men until promised relief of changed fate delivers them to men such as Orlando, husband, and the rightful Duke Senior, father—"you aren't overcome by these fantasies?" I cautioned her.

"It's prophetic, my darling," Grace whispered to me, "that you are my Orlando, the youth who rescued me from banishment, as if my father were Frederick, the usurper, who wished for sons and got girls—"

"I think you have the two Dukes confused—"

"—not at all! My father's implacable Dutch genes drove Philomena to a convent, and me to you: neither of us would become a lawyer in his sprawling firm of designated husbands. Neither of us was made that way! I was made for the life I have with you—a profession I love, daughters—"

"—*and a younger man!*" I pulled her down to the blanket as the actors took their bows. It was ten, and the summer light withheld its last firmament, we both marveled, as we held our girls between us, the crumbs of macaroon and the white foam of Guinness on our lips while we kissed.

Another day—*any day*—we set out in our stout Rover for Blenheim Palace nearby, birthplace of Winston Churchill, but passed by its glories for a much simpler country estate further north: Bedingbrough Hall. Here we took tea in a spacious park centered around an enormous tree of unfamiliar roots and name. Again, the twins were asleep on a blanket. I the budding scientist, penned a *terza-rima* for my bride of three years—:

Painted on cow-slipped landscape,
the Tree is merely etched,

converging where knowledge might emanate—;

There I stroked lamb's ear and stretched;
stood in a new pose,
my soul beckoned, fetched

lavender to my nose
as porcelain-plumed
steam from tea arose.

—Our conversation resumed,
breath embracing time,
from the moment consumed

in memory, its gaps sublime—
her cup is suspended,
hand cupped about mine—

always less than intended,
still it catches the heart:
on this we forefend—:

"The tour begins at four; shall we start?"
she asks, smile filled with scone
as we stand slightly apart,

though I am suddenly alone,
adoring her arm, pointing
where the garden is shown

in well-tilled, deep-anointed
groves of illisum, coral-bell,

tall-standing mint earthly jointed

to the spot which swells
beneath her step
as she turns and says: "All's well."

"I'm astonished!" she cried," rising from the same tea table to hold me in a swaying certitude as if we were figure skaters in an extravagant *pas de deux.* "How is it you write poetry, my genius engineer? As we were dozing over tea and the warm April sunset—was I awake?—you wrote this? Did I say those words, and cup your hands as you wrote?"

"I *observe,* darling, day and night, and this week it's our birthdays—you twenty five, I twenty two. And I do spend time at Blackwell's in the poetry aisle! Doesn't it seem we're much closer in age than when we met? I could explain it in physics: I'm catching up with you, soon to grow far and away older!"

"If I'm getting younger, my liege, it may be time to go home. Boston has a way of bringing people into their own time-zone, as if they never left, and would always return: it's more an eternal city than Rome—yes?"

"If we're finished here, let's take our British subjects to be citizens!"

Before we left Oxford, she became famous in a lecture about the roots of impressionism in art and literature, where she gave an extended abstract of a thesis she would later develop into her doctorate at Harvard. In its earliest imprimatur, she rehearsed for me the genesis of her dissertation in a breath-taking few lines:

Many scholars today unaccountably fail to draw the long-revealed artistic connection—even the birth of impressionism—between J.M.W. Turner and William Blake, who died in 1827—the year after Turner painted "Harbour of Dieppe." Both men's sense of prophecy in their art embraced wholly the conflict of imagination with reason. One hundred years later, Roger Fry, in "Vision and Design" (William Clowes & Sons, London: 1926) showed us how the "blots and blurs" in both men's art evolved directly into the work of the emigrés from the Manet Salon of French impressionism who exhibited independently between 1874 and 1886. In their quest for the infinite in art and nature, both men would not be deceived by the "rotten rags of memory disguising itself as inspiration in poetry, music and art" nor "draw [their] symbols falsely from theology and alchemy" but rather "flowers of Spring and leaves of Summer." (per Yeats). Turner, like Blake, was "not modeling after any symbols but his own: these symbols always have an inner relatedness that leads us from the outer world to the inner man." (Alfred Kazin, in his introduction to "the Portable Blake" (Viking, 1946). When I look at Regulus at the Tate, I am mindful that throughout the suffering in Blake's life, "there is always the call to us to recover our lost sight. (Kazin, Ibid.); then, in a moment linking of the two artists' spiritual reconcilement Blake says, "Men are admitted in to Heaven not because they have curbed & govern'd their Passions, or have no Passions, but because they have cultivated their Understandings." If we look between the lines in Blake's or any poet's work, and search the spaces suggested yet omitted in Turner's effusive pictures—the paint beneath the paint—We shall arrive at the interior intimacy not offered by realist painters, and prepare ourselves to trace its course trough twentieth-century literature, from Flaubert and Virginia Woolf to Katherine Mansfield and Faulkner."

"It is as sleek and refined, yet revolutionary, as any proof, theorem or postulation I have attempted," I cried out to her when I read it and the next day heard her lecture at Bodleian Library, my voice for the first time lost in a maw of admirers I did not know. She was swept away in a conclave of scholars looking for bright, undiscovered celebrity within a one-thousand-year-old university, founded by Henry II to compete with the Sorbonne, which constantly, quietly excavated its discoveries and left its remissions in a very deep vault. Whoever came across its millennial transept would find his own suppositions or inquiries discarded in time.

Grace fell rapidly away from this history and her ambitions—fell into my arms, her pure scientist who was choking in his own discoveries. "We've learned too much here," I told her. "It has overcome us. At home, we'll adopt a *slower method*—I'll take my place at Fairchild, fulfill Jocelyn's dream of moving the firm to California—this place which is replacing Route 128. You'll be with the girls, and make your mark—"

"After Oxford has made me a ghost?" she wailed. "All

my work has been dropped into a vault centuries before my time—It's happened before, and beyond—yours accelerates as fast as you grasp its meaning!"

"Darling, I merely plod along, stooping blindly for clues which lead to evidence which has to be refined by a thousand filters before I know anything of value. *Value?* You have it in your veins, and offer inspiration to a world of beauty I can only behold at an impossible distance. We have to scatter ourselves, fly away to the moment we met and pledged our future to each other, at Orient Point, and return as the man and woman we have found: Our footsteps will be hesitant and tender, and our voices forgiving: what may become of us along the way is *none of our business!*"

"Oh my darling, *my god!* Take me to bed before evening arrives!" It had never been less, and never else than a blessing ordained by the Gods!

It was my father's wit sailed us home together from Cherbourg, along with his Thérèse and my younger step-brothers, Thierry and Francis—we actually met them in South Hampton on HMS Queen Elizabeth, only two or three years before it mysteriously sank in Hong Kong Harbor—; he knew Grace and I were in a brilliant muddle: having emerged as shining adults in every way, we could not be left to drift back into our childhood. He stayed close by as we danced in the high, tapestry-hung salons, huddled on the boat deck for mid-morning beef broth, and his young boys made quick work of looking after our twins. We were nourished and restored to the fine sympathy in our life—: there was a new *bon accord.*

Such therapy allowed us to regain the crossing we had made on this ship a decade before, 1959 when we were thirteen and sixteen, with our parents—*sans ma mère*—and her sister Philomena and mine. It was the foundation of what became of our lives, and led us to our declarations at Orient Point three years later—our exquisite fidelity.

"Mclean Hospital was Joclyn's idea—do you know it's the oldest such establishment in the country, founded in 1820?—he's been there—"

"Admitted as a patient?" Grace and I gasped at the same moment.

"That's why everyone's glad you're back—to take the reins. He had something of a breakdown a month ago—mother calls it a *collapse,* as if it were the flu—because, for all his success and foresight to date, he could not see clearly where the company is going. Just as your grandfather, in the 'fifties was certain we should sell the mills and go into electronics out on 128, Jock knows this is time to move the company to California, where Hewlett Packard and Intel and others are. Son—you must take over his negotiations with Howard Hughes who wants to buy 49% of Fairchild for $200 million—he's flush from selling TWA for over a half-billion."

"But I can make us worth one billion in ten years. Actually I can dilute Hughes's shareholding—he's an expert at losing money even as he gets richer—because he knows his businesses, but doesn't know ours!"

"Are we going to see uncle Jock at the hospital now, before we go home?" Grace rewove the conversation back towards our arrival.

"He wants you to meet his doctor, share the recovery so to speak, and, if I may say so, as I suggested on the boat, have you discuss your lives with Dr. Williams as well—a kind of transition to your lives here."

"I though we did that on the Queen Elizabeth—you were superb, dad, as was your whole family! Yes, I'll take the reins, as you say and kick Fairchild in its *stifle,* if that's what it takes after all of Jock's innovations. And my wife, here, will be off to Harvard to get her PhD. in Art History— and we'll have arrived at a better sanctuary than *McClean Hospital*–!"

We found ourselves taken to McClean Hospital in Belmont in a blizzard of arrival, disorientation and retreat from our best, clever defenses with which we had pledged to each other—equipped ourselves—for the ocean voyage to survive; and believed to have left behind in Oxford when we faced a troubled realization that the sum of evanescent experiences the past three years was greater, more elusive, than the sum of ourselves simply as a young married couple. We were dragged to and tossed about in low, unfamiliar places—taken aside, and questioned our beginnings—all for the sake of Uncle Joclyn, for dear Jock.

"Never have you lost me, never have I faltered in our love, and never wondered about another life," Grace told me as we woke very late the next day, the morning last to burn through the heavy *tulle* drapes hung like ballet costumes in my grandmother's uppermost bedroom at Charles Street. "We are home, as we have not yet been, and all is for keeps! I can't imagine what the others are trying to save us, or cure us from!" We heard our girls stirring in the next room, even jumping on their beds as they pulled the enchantment of the long voyage back into the fierce discovery of where they were—no more than an indistinguishable lighthouse along the way—a close, fecund wayside of their awakening. They soon tumbled into our capacious bed—unlike the narrow berths of HMS Queen Elizabeth—and pulled us from our passion, to their passion, to a relapse of our fears, forgiveness of theirs.

Our homecoming was tenuous—: Grandmother ailing; Jock asleep in his quandaries at McClean Hospital; and father and Thérèse without their boys off to Jacob's Pillow Dance in the Berkshires for two days as we held the house, and in it, our lives together. "We have made ourselves for this!" Grace laughed. "You have learned a craft, above all your science, how to care for me, and direct ourselves into the assistance of others—look around us! What can we have forgotten?—you have taught me, have you, I was your elder smiling down over your childhood, even at Orient Point, when I throbbed to have you, in a wife-won embrace, and you held me until your sweet maturation caught up with me and I gave myself to the bridge you offered to what we have become—*"We've pulled it off!"*

Was it too good to be true? Was there a flaw, a splinter in the statue un-noticed on the mantle, or a lapse in the close geometry we had pulled and woven together into proofs we could assure ourselves were true? We've grown older, and seen our children married, translating that blessing into an assurance we've held together as we always were—no fault lines to disturb our work and a supreme belief in ourselves which we had long ago taught each other and pulled the truth of it though the sinews we had stretched across any doubts. Her parents died long before my father and Joclyn bequeathing a legacy of furniture and a plea that we reconcile faith.

Philomina withdrew from the convent to marry an older professor of Celtic Rites and Redemption at Tufts University, barely in time for her to bear, at forty, a son. Grace assisted a midwife at the birth with a gladness I knew would present itself again at our graves. I am sixty-six and she is three years older, but beyond any measurement, beyond the exquisite selection we made of each other fifty years ago, we have steered true to our lives, and kept pace with the goals and hopefulness we set before ourselves—and then set gently aside, if they did not suit us—only to find a broader canvas, a picture of ourselves, brushstrokes we might share with the world.

"Nothing has ever changed in our lives, has it?" Grace asked me a few weeks ago as we were closing up the farm on the South Coast for the winter. Our sailboat pulled from its mooring with languid ease; potatoes dug into the soil where leeks may prosper until Easter; the sheep shorn, shelter in neighboring pens. "Nothing except the way I've grown my beard, white beyond my dreams, and you've allowed my memories to mix with your desire—" I say.

We return, eternally, to Charles Street, long after my grandmother and my Uncle Joclyn have died; My father carries on in Paris, at ninety, long annealed to our well-being. Grace and I have reached the age of approbation, as teen lovers, and have won great acclaim in our lives. Still, I hold her at night as the only bulkhead against the storm.

Pharisees at Stanford

As I arrived at Stanford University from Boston on Easter Sunday, I looked for a chapel I might attend later that day. Dressed in the same glen-plaid suit, gray with thin blue lines, and the yellow sailing tie I had worn a week before at my daughter's wedding in Cambridge, I was lost on this vast, withdrawn and sterile campus, spread over a thousand or more acres as an entitlement of a rich railroad baron to preach a gospel of his own to these barren hills —Harvard west-of-the-West, they liked to say.

Footsore from parking a half-mile away, I approached Memorial Chapel—erected and dedicated a century before by Leland Stanford's wife— expecting, as a Quaker, a quiet place of reflection. But once inside the vast, gleaming replica of a church I had seen in Venice, I was met with tides of Purcell, Bach and even Fauré in choral rehearsal for Mass. I took my seat near the back and watched crowds of Asian parents and students streaming by, taking pictures feverishly with their phones of statuary and holy glass windows depicting the Saints, the Nativity and Passion. So, Stanford was a Catholic place of learning yet, perhaps a meeting ground between Paul of Tarsus and the Pharisees as may have been overlooked at Harvard Divinity School or even the country's earliest synagogue in Newport, a sanctuary provided by Roger Williams from Massachusetts.

I had turned into Campus Drive from *Juniper Serra* to see Cond*osleeza* Rice crossing from the golf course with her clubs and laughing as if Iraq had never happened. She fell away into the dim expanse of this campus with no more memory than its protean founder. I saw, to the north of the Chapel, the sallow, mute Hoover Tower standing for nothing except a lost sentinel on this bleak, succumbing landscape. I knew only New England universities such as Brown, Harvard and Yale; *and* Oxford, closed into narrow streets and squares—dense, thronging communities, where a thousand years marked a steady, vivid embrasure of the human spirit from the time of King Henry 2nd—; what Leland Stanford thought would be an empyrean of highest learning, rigor of a Pharisee in the twentieth century, had already happened centuries before, when there were civilizations awaiting graduates to come forth to serve them.

I was bitter and lost; newly divorced, and wandering from my home in Massachusetts from my grown, flourishing children, I had come west-of-the-west to console my self with my brother, a Stanford physics 'don' and founder of a start-up to succeed our old family firm on route 128.

I bowed my head and sank into the whispers of the Fauré Requiem, and found myself soothed—or compromised?—as the sacraments were revealed at the communion table, draped in purple and gold chevrons of the faithful. *Sincere Practice,* my grandfather had told me long ago at Longfellow Friends Meeting, is "take what you need; leave the rest."

"Is there a seat free beside you?" a very pretty woman twenty or more years my junior asked, modestly smoothing out the soft rose and peach pallor of her silken dress in preparation to sit beside me: I did not flatter myself that I was chosen, for the pews were filled everywhere beyond the slim twenty-four inches I could offer her. She crossed herself and bowed, showing a flame of covered russet hair and wildly freckled necklines, murmuring, "I am *not* Catholic, but isn't Easter for all of us?"

"I am here for the music," I whispered. "I'll see about the Eucharist."

She sat back upright on the wooden bench, her hands folded meekly across her lap. As the Fauré ended, we stood for a Homily from the priest preparing God's table. She took my hand: "Then we'll both go forth?"

"Shall we wait for the hymn?" I asked her.

"There're won't be one, just a canticle sung by the priest—"

"—to gather us—?"

"—and......provide.....for....us...as...we...walk forward... *together*," she smiled, almost chanting.

I noticed only her shoes, in her hands, shapely summer pumps. She must have walked into the pew barefoot. "Do your shoes hurt you feet?"

She laughed softly, a wind shifting easily from North to Southwest. "They are new, yes, and pinch a bit, but I wanted to step into the church without them—pure you might say—to meet the cool tiles beneath us."

"Beneath us?"

"I saw you walk in, talking to yourself, so angry you were about to jump out of *your* shoes!" She bent to untie the laces of my white bucks.

After Communion and the final musical praises of things seen, unseen and held in abeyance for another day, we stepped out, holding our shoes, into the April sun, blazing across the concourse enclosing first structures from the rail-road man's dream. I quickly explained myself and she nodded as if she already knew this, or something like my story. "Are you too young to be a professor, or too old to be a graduate student here?" I asked her.

"I am thirty-two—opposite your fifty-two, I'd say—and an assistant professor of Am-Civ Literature & Civilization in the Twentieth Century. Would you mind tying our shoes over your shoulders, like hockey skates, slung as you may have once approached your frozen cranberry bogs?"

"How on earth would you know about that?" I shuddered.

"Silly, dear man: I was at your daughter's wedding last week! We were at Wellesley together, I two years older, and I saw you withdraw—"

"—then you've been *stalking* me—?"

"Let's say I followed you, especially as I had to return to Stanford."

"Did Fiona tell you I was coming out to see my brother?"

"Oh, everyone here in Silicon Nation knows who Seth

Fairchild is—and *who you were!* I just followed the course by celestial navigation!"

"Then, you must tell me who you are, Miss—"

"Febiger, if you can say it without stumbling. Amy Febiger."

It was she who stumbled, tripping flat upon my chest, into my arms, her arms around my waist.

"Amy—I may be still in love with my ex-wife! Are you a *Pharisee?* But I kissed her before she could say.

We were married two months later in the chapel where we met. My brother was best man and Amy's father, scowling, gave her away as he had, two years before, to her first husband the moment she graduated from Wellesley. "We are Jewish," Amy had explained two days before the wedding; "father creates a separateness, a defiance in a place like this—" she waved across the pagan Christian splendor of Stanford Chapel—"and seeks the purity in waiting for the Messiah in the first century or two after Christ." I bowed to her explanation, if not belief: She was pregnant.

We settled in a Spanish-style house in Los Altos Hills, just three or four miles from where she teaches, and I went to work with my brother in Mountain View, three or four miles the other direction. After our son was born, my daughter Fiona flew out from Boston to be with Amy, and they were close enough in age—Fiona, twenty-eight and unmarried—to bond like sisters. My brother, forty five, and I played pick-up lacrosse at Stanford but beyond

Amy's classes, which Fiona decided to audit, I took little interest in the campus except to be reminded it was the incubator of the start-up which ten years earlier had given resurrection to our family's business, Fairchild Electronics. Thirty years before, fresh out of M.I.T., I with my father negotiated a 49% sale of the company to Howard Hughes, valuing the company at $200 million. Now, 2003, it's $2 billion.

My brother and I were working to sell the company again. Howard Hughes Medical Foundation's shareholding has fallen to 20% due to our aggressive stock repurchases and acquisition of another 20% at twice book value by a foreign firm I shall not name. So we have 60%, or $1.2 billion at current valuation. With most Fairchilds now deceased, we'll give most of that to M.I.T and other schools we and our sister attended as well as endow a new marine science center at Woods Hole.

"I had no idea!" Amy exclaimed, at dinner with Fiona and her beau.

"We've lived modestly over the years, and taken very little out of the company. Before coming here, I lived in my grandmother's house in Back Bay, and we summered on the family farm on Buzzards Bay, where we sailed. We'll go there at the end of the summer: ten very old bedrooms!"

"And Ben will love it!" Fiona gestured to her man, Amy's age and introduced by Amy—he an assistant professor of mathematics and statistics at Stanford. Ben and I traded jokes about the elegance of the "Poisson Probability Distribution" and its Bernoulli trial, and especially the law of *rare events*—which I said out of Amy's hearing was like finding a devout, Talmudic Jew at Stanford. But my darling Amy would prove me wrong, for as she learned of my Quaker practice, she translated its inner light into a parallel in Judaism of forbearance and morality. Fiona and Ben were very serious and discussing a September wedding, when we'd all be back in Massachusetts. There would be robust October sailing before Amy and I returned to Los Altos to await our son's first birthday, my fifty-third, twenty years ahead of Amy.

"Have you—*we*—ever considered," Amy asked, but didn't really ask ten years later when I was sixty-three, she forty-three, and our son Solomon had been joined by his sister Leah, "what it has meant these past years since I found you in a church, a penitent like me, looking for life in all the Gospels?" She was as beautiful as the day we met, and she took me away.

"I have rarely thought about anything except you and me, where we are at any given moment, and where our steps may take us. I love you in all your guises, and simply worship the day you followed me to Stanford. I do confess that in that first year, up until Solomon was born, confusion plagued me—Ben once called it 'lines of disfigurement'—not that I was anything but stunned you'd choose an old fool like me—but that I would *question* why I found myself where I was—"

"Until you read Paul Célan's poem about Masada—*Denk Dur*—and I understood your passion of Golgotha, we were at rather an impasse, but you soon became my 'honorary

78

Jew!" She kissed me with all her youth, and murmured, "forget the diaphragm: shall we go for a third? We'll pick a Christian name, your turn after two from my tribe—"

"—I love your tribe, ever searching past certitude and coming up with new questions, always new questions, until I had to sort it out at McClean Hospital—"

"But that was so long ago, dear heart—you should have forgotten."

And if you are sixty-three and your wife is forty-three, you rush ahead and surrender your seed.

We awoke hours later still coupled together as the early morning wind from Buzzards Bay blew our curtains like spinnakers sailing into our room. As I withdrew from Amy, I left traces of semen on her thigh, its arc slung high over my waist. She stirred half-asleep to say, "bulls-eye."

We moved back to Massachusetts after my brother and I completed our sale of the company in Silicon Nation and are living down on grandmother's farm by the sea, raising sheep for wool, vegetables for road-side markets. Fiona, Ben and children are in Providence, where she teaches at Brown University; my brother lives in Charles Street, at our grandmother's house and is administering our grant to M.I.T.; Amy's father has retired to Lexington. So I tell her we are close-held in a carapace of love and longing, always renewed within not more than an hour's drive and the space of millennia so fondly rediscovered and found, awaiting our next child.

Boston Casualty

"This won't be one of your *moments of truth* will it?" my wife asked tenderly as if holding a shield up to protect me from my fragile or bitter self. "As you said yourself on the plane, a big reunion is not a ship foundering on shoals—"

"—easy for you to say at your age!"

At the end of a narrow alley off Tremont Street—near the corner of Beacon well back of the Common—we perched in a cramped, dark French-*influenced* restaurant as a gloom of constant rain met broken pavements in a sigh of regret for a dear, tired city. Having grown up in Massachusetts I was abruptly numbed to be heading to my fiftieth high school reunion at a private school down on Buzzards Bay where I would now be welcomed as an "Admiral"—neither regret nor glee—I to open my purse to coffers of endowment.

Arriving at Logan after a San Francisco flight I felt no hearing in my right ear. Believing it to be a wax built-up, I fetched hydrogen peroxide and poured it in at our hotel, lost my balance and fell to the bathroom floor in our $500 room barely refurbished from a century-old office building, dark and musty, and testing my wife's asthma like a twice-told tale with no room service, no coffee or tea—yet a small, sweet reminder of my grandmother's house down past the State House on Charles Street gave back the boundless hopefulness I'd once found across

Longfellow Bridge at M.I.T., then across California's Silicon Nation to Stanford.

"You've hurt yourself on the towel rack!" Grace exclaimed at the blood on the wall and my elbow where she sponged more peroxide, foaming the wound promiscuously as my ear bubbled in counterpoint. "Can you stand? Did you hit your head? Wait—wait—let me help you up! Everything is so shadowy here," bless her—:

We met and married over thirty years ago at Stanford, where I had gone for graduate work and then transferred my family's electronics firm from Route 128 to Silicon Peninsula south of San Francisco. Grace was a California girl, wide and wondrous of all she saw and met—even in me, a reclusive Quaker from Back Bay—and bestowed upon our twin children, Seth and Fiona, *very* non-identical.

"But darling, you always miss rain in California," Grace teased me as I growled at a broken umbrella taken from the lobby and we stumbled down the hill towards dinner. I noticed a small weathered plaque set in the hotel entrance stone which read *Boston Casualty*, the name of an old insurance company my grandfather used long ago: seeing the hotel's provenance I picked up my steps and snapped:

"Probably due to your entitled need of constant sunshine in a drought-state with narry a plan to desalinate oceans of water—"

"Oh, it eventually rains, and next year, *el niño*—"

"—will bring mud slides next year and fires the next! I begin to think we should finally move back here—"

"—tell you what my darling, Solomon-of-the-ancients: your reunion is four days of golf, drinking and fund-raising:

we'll spend two and the weekend down at the farm—sail, clambake with Liz—"

"—she's in France with André, for the seventieth anniversary of D-Day—our father and his—*how I miss my sister.*"

"*And remember,* darling fiftieth, this is the hundredth anniversary of your school's schooner—al-a-tauto!—and you *admirals* get your own sail Thursday morning. Now tell me again about that dear boat's history..."

"One hundred foot keel; built as Dutch pilot boat in 1914 and captured by the Germans as a training ship; given to the school in 1950 by my uncle Joclyn—Jock—and named *Buzzards Bay Boy.*"

"Full marks!" she laughed. I pulled her waist against me, so slender across a decade, my sixty-eight to her fifty-eight—what a blessing!

Next day it rained again in rare, angry quadrants from the Bay and I found Guinness and we left at three and met the exodus from Boston down Routes 93 and 24—less than the terrible flight from Paris to Tour of June, 1950, André's parents suffered—with no rest stops for ninety minutes: I simply had to release my bladder upon the seat of the rental car and sit in a warm, then freezing pool of sterile, I assured myself, urine. We arrived at the gentle swell and farmlands of the Southcoast before six. I showered, dressed in the school's blazer and arrived at the Headmaster's dinner for admirals just in time to receive a badge and greet classmates I did not recognize, save for their badges.

In the morning, awakening from snug student bunks, we walked from the village across the sea-facing campus where bright chevrons were suspended everywhere to mark classes from five to fifty years, in qincennial leaps, as flags flew for every sport and as banners of school history. As eight bells rang, we boarded the schooner for our afternoon sail. Anchor up, engines engaged purely to leave the busy harbor. Out in the Bay, as we took our places on deck, mizzen and main rose with powered winches and surprised jibs flapped with alacrity into a starboard reach towards the shallow hills of Falmouth. An aroma of steaming chowder arose from the galley below, and ale and cheese were set out in the wardroom—the pilot house. At the helm the Captain was joined by his exec, a senior girl shouting orders to the linesmen as top gallants flew with my heart: Is this too good to be true...? This is the school where my life began!

We slept in student housing, formerly private summer cottages, dreaming of our sail back, Grace leaning into my assured arms, past and future vanished as we claimed six-foot swells downwind from Woods Hole. Doubled up, the bunks were snug, and sparse blankets held us in an embrasure of youthfully coiled loins in safety we had not felt in years—yet I felt also a sudden fear climb the back of my spine, as if a coil of reason had escaped its natural tension and relapsed into a boundary I could never grasp.

Breakfast was served beneath a huge, white phantom tent: muffins, juice and coffee—no protein—but we had the day ahead for grilled cod or haddock, even *finnan haddie?* NO: beef, chicken and their barbequed ruins. In the afternoon the wind came up and halyards on masts and flagpoles were screaming my overlooked name. I bent my footsteps towards the library to look into class archives, arrayed across glass cases like specimens showing other views from the past from one hundred fifty years. Grace—I refused to know her meaning—'texted' our children in California and I knew she had summoned them east. I turned away and threw my phone into the harbor, after calling my long-ago roommate to meet behind the library with his provender of marijuana.

Leaving the library, I fell into a mood of a wanderer, free of any indicated future. Along a path, which divided in a direction I had lost, I met the Director of Development who wanted to talk less about a mere check and more about a *bequest.* Beneath early maples and oaks, we sat on a memorial bench: "You can include the school in your will or give a gift now for which we'll pay an annuity until your death," he advised me cheerfully as I searched over our estate's elasticity to give. True, it was very abundant—:

—and it was true I loved the school like my life—

A new promise of life at fourteen emerged following four years of tyranny in the grip of Fairchild School, founded by my great grandfather in 1900 and nominated by Harvard philosopher George Santayana as a "hotbed of cruelty and snobbery" in his 1936 novel *The Last Puritan.* My grandfather Seth Fairchild left the school in more secular hands to sell the family textile mills and found Fairchild Electronics near Wellesley on Route 128. After graduating from Buzzards Bay Academy in 1964, I headed to M.I.T. to fulfill granddad's dream of my stepping in for my late father—he and mother were lost in the sinking of *Andrea Doria* in 1956 off Nantucket—to someday lead the fledgling company. I remember racing with the fleet of Laser-twos in the Charles and reclining along Memorial Drive with a girl who turned out not to be Grace: my path to Stanford found her one Christmas listening to the Fauré Requiem in the Memorial Chapel pressed into possibly the last two available seats. We married there two months later.

"**D**id you say something, my darling?" she murmured as we lay naked on the dock at the river bending alongside grandmother Fairchild's farm which my twin sister Lisbeth and I had inherited from our parents tragic estate. I had set our Marshall 22 catboat in its mooring and we swam the incoming Slocums tide before it shifted its elbow into the Paskamansett, an estuary drawing herring fleeing before bluefish—both eyed by great blue heron waiting in the marsh grasses. Away from my school and its superannuated merriment and awaiting the arrival of our children from California at Logan in the evening, we pulled ourselves wearily from the current upon the dock and fell into the wide embrace of middle-'fifties love-making—spooling our memories and gladdened to arch our backs and hips in perfect, lean torque, and pinion our legs, firm as they had been before the twins were born—Grace, astride me sang out, "is it possible I just felt your semen reach my cervix after years of hesitant approach?" I arched upwards so that she fell backwards into my arms and opened her silks of girlhood to my mouth—something I had not attempted in a long time—and I thought I heard her cry out, "It's too good to be true!" This saddened me amidst a moment of gladdened tidings—

But we began to prepare dinner for our children's arrival *au bon accord*—as André would often say about life with Liz—cod and scallops fresh from the New Bedford fleet for chowder Rhode Island style, from broth, white wine, leeks and potatoes found in high cupboards and cold cellar from the winter, all with a favorite California adaptation: red Thai curry paste and coconut milk. The first June legumes, peas and beans, strung themselves along old wires and poles. The cottage with its ten bedrooms was not heated, but we would light a broad woodstove well before the kids arrived to spill heat into the downstairs sitting and dining rooms as the late Spring night wove a surprising chill after our warm hours on the mid-day water. And a late Southeast wind came up the river to shake the halyards into a weaving promise of good sailing the next day. A few strands of family, and the far-away sounds of past life wandered up the hill.

"I can only hear what I have left behind and not found these days," I answered our kids' questions about the reunion. Doubtfully I continued: "I see myself as an outcast, yes, a cast-aside pilgrim abandoned by my tribe, all vanished, my disfigured past claiming treachery as I sold the family firm to others; left my bearings and surrendered my sad progeny from their legacy—a quilt woven in loss—"

"—*however can you say that?*" Grace tempted my submission to a generation waiting at home. "Your *fête champêtre* at your school is done—a fine reunion collapsed in the myth you have held aloft for fifty years—within which, dear heart, you blessed me for a lifetime! And what a success you've been: Sold Fairchild twice, which we find prospers as a pubic company!"

"Forgive me, Grace: I *want* to settle here, sell out in Los Altos. We'll have eighty acres, enough for sheep to be shorn, and dogs to chase into our close hillocks beyond. And if I give the school a million, it will maintain the schooner for years, and a building with another million with my name on it will keep *them* away—away from my doubt, away from my last hope—"

"—which began two hours ago, on the dock—"

"Then I'd better give it all away, banish it, shave myself for eternity before I'm caught. *No,* I'll wait for Liz, she owns half—my true love, can't you see—and has been since we were children, orphans: She'll know what to do and where to go—can you see?" Ask what happens when *things fall apart*—"

"We'll find gifts of asking, listening, pondering."

My sister returned from France with André two weeks after I was admitted to McClean Hospital in Belmont—the oldest mental health institution in the country, founded 1820—I was proud to be there—where grandmother and I had taken her husband at his collapse when his reason unwound itself in fast-fading garlands of memory and regret after my parents died at sea. His son was lost in the War. My uncle Joclyn had not married, and there were no young women left until he saw mother's sister waiting in the silence in the Longfellow Friends Meeting in Cambridge twenty years ago, when Grace and I had been married twenty years—can it be forty years since Grace was eighteen and I a near twenty-eight?—Doctor, how, where, have I missed inauguration and dispensation I expected to carry me ahead, not leave me aside, abandoned—?

"He is not lucid just now," Grace told Lisbeth as they sat outside his room in a sheltered alcove, very nearly a chapel-of-ease, "but he's been making plans in his own way, as he always has in California. From his staggering promises to his school they want to make him trustee—a bit sudden, given his outlook— and the children are here to moderate the outcome. Mere money is not a question and his sagacity has been something of a lapsed sounding board as far as lawyers can see. Stanford naturally hopes to keep a hand in—pledges to be redeemed from a company spawned on its vast domain—no: everything will go to M.I.T. for the Joclyn School of Engineering."

I awoke to many sounds, effluents of converging streams of all the promises I had made upon waking just days ago when my sister and wife walked me from the hospital grounds as a spear of light fell through the trees to measure my steps, an easy prologue to where I was headed. Larks, finches and martins sang in their tripartite processions I had never anticipated as we, grounded, flew over the lanes to Boston, a redeemer, yet a casualty pinning me to a past I could not redeem or discard, then on to our sanctuary on the South Coast.

"Are you safe and settled?" Grace asked as we approached the farm. "There is no airplane, hidden passageway or planetary disorder ahead: Our two children and their children are standing on the dock, already returned from sailing and the safety of everything we have found."

"Then we are exactly where we began," I agreed with a sleek familiarity with what she was saying yet fell short of hearing a benediction I had wished.

—Marion, Massachusetts: June, 2014

We shall not cease from exploration, and the end of all our exploring will be to arrive where we started and know the place for the first time. _T.S. Eliot

Jacob's Pillow

The only sound reason Geoffrey could imagine his grandmother would not encourage his visit at Thanksgiving to the old family farm in Hamilton, Massachusetts—almost close enough to hear the polo balls *chuckered* at Myopia Hunt Club—was that he had married immediately upon his first wife's death three months before. What came to light soon enough was that Geoffrey and Geraldine had been married in his first wife, Julia's hospital room, where she was fast succumbing to pancreatic cancer—a sudden, swift and merciless ailment that took her away in six weeks—and the hospital chaplain was told Julia was a sister. As she died three days later, the newlyweds achieved impunity.

"But Gran," Geoffrey tried to reason, "Julia *asked* us to marry—in her sight: 'My cousin is the only woman for you to have', she told us. And, as Julia was Catholic, and given the setting, it would have been unseemly to conduct a divorce—"

"The whole affair is *unseemly*—since you selected the word—I can't imagine cousin Geraldine acceding. *Unless*—"

"Yes. Geraldine is expecting—also encouraged by Julia—"

"Infamy!" his grandmother proclaimed—for she rarely spoke in any other tongue—; yet, beneath her pale cream *tulle* and cobalt gown, and a diadem she wore on all such occasions since grandfather had brought it home from the Crimea, she smiled.

Then Thanksgiving was upon them—family coming from every quadrant of the Commonwealth: Dartmouth, Ipswich, Winchester, far-off Sandisfield, Duxbury, Dedham, Wellesley, Woburn, Wareham, even Springfield and Sudbury—was it?—and Milton. It was a dense yet far-flung coruscation of namesakes and place-names from over two centuries of Fairchild natives, with some interposing Tripp Quakers from Westport added in.

"Have you gathered rockweed from the river?" she scolds always the youngest she can throw against the task of building the beds for a lobster and clambake—turkeys were forever free to wander the forests of tupelo and cedar which thronged her acreage—with the last of the corn and red potatoes thrown into the embers late in the day. Geraldine has made pies, shyly lining them up for inspection on the long table devoted to the memory of provender gathered freely in October: sour apple, surly quince, concord grape from the river; sweet potato—not mere pumpkin—and the last traces of rose hips from the beach which she resolved into a roux with ricotta that fell into a crushed almond crust like penitents before an altar.

Geoffrey hung back, not knowing if his young, approved wife would meet the test of his grandmother's standards: his parents had perished long ago in a shipwreck his grandmother had not fully accepted—but there it was, from 1956, *Andrea Doria*—the bodies lay in the deeps of Nantucket Bay.

And he had grown up in her house from the age of

ten—he was a day student at a prominent boy's school outside Boston, and later a boarding student at another school on the other side of Boston—and then for college, fled down to Brown in Providence, where he met Julia. They married a week after graduation, along the Rappahannock River in Virginia, where her family were. Now, 1986, he was forty and Gran was ninety and running on all twelve cylinders, she would say, recalling grandfather's 1956 Packard, in which he was buried, sitting at the wheel, twenty feet below a grove of holly and cedar at the rear of acreage, diminished since the funeral ten years ago.

"My dear Geraldine—do they call you *Gerry?*— I hope not—I love the festive imagination in your baking! You've been down at the shore to gather all this, haven't you? But of course you have, Geoffrey took you sailing out of Padanaram. Pretty sturdy wind on Buzzards Bay, this time of year, and very *changeable* my husband always said, *wickedly so!*"

"Thank you—Gran," she blushed and turned to look at her new husband, but she was on her own: he was laughing with a cousin in another room, probably about another time. "If we have a boy, we'd like to name it after Geoff's grandfather," she continued hopefully and the face she saw beamed Gran's love.

"My darling girl, whatever for?" "*Seth* is so wooden, stiff—well, more gentle than *Josiah!*"

"Oh—I think it has a simple musical line," Geraldine offered, forgetting Gran was speaking of a burial in a Packard.

"Something with three syllables, from the Old Testament, would be nice: Joshua, Solomon or Benjamin—"

"My grandfather had four: Na-than-i-al—"

"—*perfect*, right out of our woods!" Gran cried rising from her chair to embrace Geraldine. "Now, you're an art historian?"

"I actually work as a curator," the young woman stepped quickly into the freshened pace of the conversation. "The Peabody."

"Ah...Salem," Gran whispered as from a reverie, "... *Essex.*"

"And I've taken on organizing the education department," Geraldine spoke more assuredly. "Working with high schools."

"Did you meet my grandson here in Boston?"

"No—didn't he tell you? We met at a modern dance performance."

"Jacobs Pillow? In the Berkshires?" Gran seemed to know.

"Yes!" Geraldine stammered. "Last summer: Paul Taylor. Geoffrey took me for coffee at intermission, bought me ballet shoes and told me about the Underground Railway at Pillow."

"Dear girl, modern dance is in my blood. I met Ted Shawn soon after he started it, in the 'thirties. I studied with him and later danced with the company until I met Seth, my husband. I was forty. Ted and I were lovers for a year before, and we had a daughter. Seth adopted her and she married Geoffrey's father."

"**Y**ou and Gran have finally bonded!" Geoffrey

exclaimed as he found Geraldine in the kitchen, stacking the dishwasher and setting the remains of the turkey in a large pot of water, carrots and celery. There were still murmurs of approval from her table of desserts. Gran had long gone up to bed, kissing Gerry in a long farewell: she called her Geraldine and waved from a stairway.

"She and I declared a love of each other. She told me your history, and about your grandfather in the Packard out back—"

"—oh *that*," he laughed guardedly. "He drove it into the sea up in Maine, twenty years ago. I was in college—with Julia."

"Yes, my cousin. I know that part. Gran said he died ten—"

"—a favorite myth: you must know this family *thrives*—"

"—*on myths?*" she rushed into the colloquy with sleek assurance that her husband did not know of his ancestry— or, in an eclipse of sensibility, had invented a story even his late wife had not believed at Geraldine's wedding in the hospital.

"At least I'm an open book," he laughed, taking her away from the soup pot and the dishes into arms. "We have help for all this, somewhere in the house. I can't remember, truthfully."

Guarding her condition, they made love gently that night with her above him. All was restored, and as she climaxed, she called out the names Gran had supplied— "Joshua, Solomon—!"

Geoffrey was more surprised by Gran's will than Geraldine. The entire estate was left to Jacob's Pillow Dance, to build a new theatre and endow the school. The old house she left *adjoint* to Geoffrey and Geraldine for their *married lifetime*, and afterward to their son, Nathanial, or daughter un-named, as the following months would disclose. It was very exact and good-natured, as those thing go.

Geraldine wanted to dig up the Packard and place Gran inside beside the remains of her husband until Geoffrey, taking possession of the homestead, took her to the barn and showed her the trussed-up remains of the car, which had been towed back from the frigid waters off Mount Desert Island. "His body was never found," was all he said. "Now, off to the junkyard."

They moved immediately, from his top-floor apartment in an old bow-faced town house in Back Bay, walking distance from his law practice, but they would halve the distance of her commute to Salem to eight miles until the baby came. But she wanted to work there afterwards. They knew from her tests it would be a boy, so Nathanial was carved into the testamentary book of his future. "Can we sell the house now?" she asked, "and move someplace smaller. Just the land is worth a fortune!"

"No, angel, no need. I'm a partner now. We'll be fine here."

And so they settled into the homestead of his patrimony.

Just before Nathanial was born, she read the famous line from Tolstoy: "All happy families are alike; each unhappy family is unhappy in its own way." She never got much further than the advent of Anna's affair with Count Vronsky. It sickened her—a dread of the arc and *embrasure* of the story rose up—and she saw her life divided between two old families: Julia's in Virginia and Geoffrey's in Massachusetts—poor Geraldine a discarded relation.

Later, in the hospital, the baby at her breast and Geoffrey beside, she forgot—set apart—everything Gran had said. Yet long hours alone with Nathanial while his father worked at his law practice and scouted the possibilities to run for elected office—Gran's husband, Geoffrey's grandfather, had been governor for one term in the late 'fifties—pulled Gerry, as everyone called her now, into a fragile reverie of her husband's legitimacy and therefore her own. What Gran had told her had never been disclosed to Geoffrey, that he was Ted Shawn's true grandson and not Seth Fairchild's. With the loss of his parents at ten, the history from Jacobs Pillow went down off Nantucket.

"Darling, you've never told me much about your parents," she said as he took her home from Beth Israel Deaconess two days later. "I know you said farewell, but what were they like?"

"I can't really remember. He was an engineer from M.I.T."

"And she was at Radcliffe, Gran told me. Where did you live when you were a young boy?"—she felt herself asking as his mother—"and what did you do the summer they were in—"

"Italy. She'd won an internship at the Uffizi, in Florence. I stayed the summer with my father's family in Truro, on the Cape." He gripped the wheel firmly and ran his thumbs around its rim as he fixed his eyes upon the trusses of the Mystic River Bridge as if he thought it might collapse. He exhaled relief audibly as they met Route One, the road home. "Let's just leave it behind us, sort of like the *afterbirth* they took away from Nathanial. I've thought about what you suggested—selling the Hamilton place—and I think the time is right. I don't feel connected to it as I used to. A friend over at State Street Bank has a client who's eager to find property there, or in Beverly, but our land beats the North Shore hands down. The house is two centuries old, and we've done nothing to it, but they won't pull it down!"

"You've met these people?" she asked, curling her baby.

"Friends of Seth and Gran. I can get us around the will—"

"—that we have to live there, married, all our lives?"

"—*I want a life with you*—not a mausoleum! Sometimes I felt my parents were buried there, and not at sea! No, we'll sell, and the money can finance my campaign and all of our lives!"

He had saved himself! She laughed all the way home—but still held to a regret for the lost Packard.

A Second Reading

I came to a tumbling halt before a musty shelf in a beloved, out-of-print bookstore somewhere along Newbury Street—maybe it was Bolyston—not far from my twin sister's gallery when I returned to Boston after my years in California. Repentance and regret for leaving Massachusetts surged through my veins, even—I saw helplessly—without my mother's reminder of my misplaced life. I stared at a title from 1955 almost erased from the worn, mildewed cover, and saw that the author, Sloan Wilson—whose novel, *The Man in the Gray Flannel Suit* had been made into a movie with Gregory Peck—was the father of a girl I had fallen in love with in college, and lived with my senior year off-campus. We had planned to marry after graduation. Somewhere in the late Spring we grew blithe about birth control and she became pregnant: in 1968, when so much of our daily world bore tarnished meaning—Vietnam, the killing of Robert Kennedy, Dr. King, and the mendacity of public life—; we were delighted to be expecting.

Her father, preparing a screenplay for another novel in Hollywood, rose from his dramatic stupor and came to take his daughter west to have my child. She disappeared, as if taken in a lowering fog in the marshes along the river by my family home where I came to console myself throughout the failures in my life. But Lily was not a failure! She had upheld, like a bright chevron, a vision of our married life together, even at twenty, and pledged fidelity.

I took up her father's books with a vengeance, found nothing of Lily in its pages, and vowed to take his name into literary purgatory—one of Dante's circles—and made them part of a PhD 'dissertation of disaffection' as my adviser mused.

A few years later, when I gained a platform of rebuke, tenure at Tufts University—never Harvard, where I was an idle undergraduate—I was sufficiently poised to suffer the *slings and arrows of outrageous fortune* to reach the hearth-stone of my discontent: Truth and Valor: Publish.

"What possible academic merit can you achieve by attacking a very ordinary novel written thirty years ago?" one of my colleagues asked at a mid-term lull when the faculty relapsed into idle gossip and affairs with their students—male and female. "Are you infected with some aspect of Wilson's life which you must bring to the attention of the world?"

"What an implausible name—like Franchette Tone, the actor, if you can remember such a mateneé idol—but the less you think about errant personalities rather than principles, the more you'll gather yourself into a place of sensible acceptance." He went on for some time, but his remarks never became less opaque than 'sensible acceptance' where he lost me and I fled the hollow, abandoned faculty lounge. Two years later, I enrolled at M.I.T. to fulfill my family's expectations of leading our Firm!

Our early undergraduate courtship had been formal and elegant: dinners, high teas, and my attending her athletic program, gymnastics. She came to my lacrosse games and squash-rackets matches; when I went to college, I'd given up playing hockey on frozen cranberry bogs on the Massachusetts South Coast. If I went out for three sports at college, I would have no time for my beloved Lily and, I soon discovered, no time for drinking which, in years of boarding schools, I had never attempted—save for pressing grapes into bottles with yeast which exploded in my dresser drawer: my undershorts were pink, a transformation I never explained changing in the locker room. In college, my drinking template became dry martinis before dinner, and Guinness at lunch with a salad and Double Gloucester cheese—the magic meal, like paella, full of mystery, nourishment and rare spices, even unfamiliar textures, octopus hidden in saffron grains—.

Lily laughed in a rousing, boasting yet shy manner, and called my attempts at *haute cuisine* in our small undergraduate apartment in Somerville 'Much Ado about Nothing.' I called her my Beatrice—not from Shakespeare but the soul of Dante's *Paradisio*—and saw in her my rising light, my moments of returning, like Peer Gynt to his Solveig. She read Ibsen's play slavishly to find my meaning, and at the end lay back on our narrow bed and pulled me into her for a close reconciling of what I'd said: "Does that say you will wander the world endlessly, be a munitions supplier, and end up in a mental institution before you can come back to me?"

"Not at all: I shall be with you always, as I am now, never far away—never closer."

Before I graduated, and her father took her away to three years of exile in California, we dismissed any baleful outlook. Then I said we must marry to provide an adhesive for our lives: Go out into the world as a team, more than a couple, strike at an anvil of the future we saw ahead; anneal ourselves to our dreams and hopes—a leap we both wished to make, yet had no idea where we would land—except to fall weightlessly back into the soft cushions of care for each other we had patiently cultivated for years. Then I went off to my exams and she was left with morning sickness at nineteen and separate—a winnowing of her spirit to the floorboards of our life together. "Help!" Lily would call out at improbable moments, usually when she was alone. She pulled on despair and sought her father, a bitter widower.

"Could we come back together in our thirties, forties or middle age? Is there another corridor we could walk where, when God closes one door, he opens another—but there is hell in the hallway?" she pleaded as I began to dread a future without her, or—my—child: it was an unspeakable speculation, and I fell into days and nights of remorse and punishment, and held her closer in bed than I had ever envisioned or had given myself to imagine. Yet there was a pull away from me, she hid herself in quandaries of seclusion, and asked to see her father, to verify her life with him, and his work. Lily faded into an opprobrium of doubt, an abstinence which was foreign to her bright nature. Her father, the great author, came and took her away, his insolence masked by cheerful duplicity as he promised her a new life in California. He knew not how it would unfold, and they left without a compass, yet his contempt for me was unbridled.

As much as fell into an unexplained space, just that portion was given to revival and reunion as the years passed and great distances spread their canopy over Lily's and my lives. We seemed protected, sheltered from the harm we had done each other; world without end was, at best, compromised. We had not married. A few years later, when she made a visit with our young daughter, she surprised me on two counts: First, she wanted to stay with me and sleep with me; second, she woke up early after a night of renewed love-making and shouted, "I'll not be a character in one of my father's books!" Another of his was made into a silly movie with Sandra Dee. "You never could be, they're too boring," I assured her. She stayed in Boston month after month until she became pregnant again, now a mere twenty-two.

I had been blessed with the inheritance of my grandmother's slender, tall house in Charles Street, steps from the Common; an entry position as a college associate professor would never have provided an income to live in such a prestigious location. Lily loved it, and we were married quietly at the Longfellow Friends Meeting House in Cambridge. My family had been Quakers for two centuries, and had prospered first with textile mills and then, in the 1950's, starting an electronics firm out along the fledgling technology campus known as Route 128. My father, Seth Fairchild, had been to M.I.T. and taken his studies into the world and left us, eventually, very well-off, especially after my brother took the firm in the 'seventies to a place called Silicon Valley in California, while I soldiered on in Boston.

We woke to the sounds of our children racing between rooms and hiding themselves in secure fenestrations in the house—alcoves, dumb waiters and the searing intent of others who waited in silences for the true benevolence of how we—Lily and I—pulled each other into the gradual, sharp and dutiful admission of our lives: We walked in through windows, glazed against morning light; we crept into familiar pantries and storerooms where I had hidden myself as a child, peering into the outer world for suggestions; finding none, I fled to the cellars and hid myself from the awful heritage I had been expected to present: perhaps a Fairchild curse—the sneaking suspicion that somewhere, someone was happy—she dismissed it.

"Whatever we dig up here, you are all perfectly safe: we'll excavate the future, never the past," she assured me. "It's left us, whatever it was, in a smaller sphere, a need to flee backwards into our last testaments." She eased herself over to me and fell into an embrace which my mother could not have envisaged, or her husband's Puritan tribe ordained.

The moment left me and my beloved Lily soon floundering in Boston, the remnants of fireworks still landed on their street, and floods of people pushed them aside to gain a foothold on the pavements that would bring them back the sweet garden and home. Lily turned toward me as she had never found a moment to display: "There has never been a moment like this when you gave me freely what I had given you—" I waved away the shadow around her.

"Is that why your father's love trumped mine—why he took you and our child from me?" I demanded, to put a clear window in the thick air between us.

"You could have followed your brother! But I'm here now, and we've had another child!" she pleaded.

"And I stayed here the three years you were there—in purgatory!"

"So, are you rehearsing some grievance from the past to play itself out in the future? You can't be that much of a prisoner—even as jailor!"

In steady gradations, I felt myself withdraw from the precipice I had created, the sheets of ice on the mountain I had expected to cross to find my life and first and only love. She was there to meet me at each of the elevations I must descend from the impossible altitude I set for myself to climb: "I feel like I'm falling," I cried suddenly, "that I've let go of all my ropes and belays and splints in the rocks where there are no rocks, just a smooth, shining face of a mountain with no saving ledges—"

"—then you must let me catch you—as you always have: let go—"

"Are you sure, my angel? How would I do that without my past, and where will I go to find what lies ahead? I feel I've so little time left to—"

"You have all the time in the world," she assured me: "Today!" Again we heard footsteps running over the wide old boards of grandmother's farmhouse.

Of course, the reader will surmise, we stepped back from the precipice, which was never there at the start. We annealed these wounds—accepted them as not of our making, and could easily forgive ourselves, like children leaving a bad dream—; a moment of awakening from such a dream was filled with alternative phantoms, then the soft opening of eyes to the world as it is, or is to be.

An immense canopy of safety spread over the day, making ordinary events come to life in stunning relief: the breakfast table, with its shining plates and silver racks of toast; the poached eggs, sitting magically upon razor-thin slices of ham; a bowl of berries and fruits from the garden, as if the trees and bushes had offered a blessing, as soft as Lily's kiss upon each of the girls' brows, huddled in a smirking conclave between them as they wondered at the food presented, and made plans for the day.

"What shall do today?" Lily called out brightly, as if tucking away in her flowing summer dress the passion of last night's love-making and presenting a renewed face to our children—a face of patient surmise—; I gathered my family into a wide embrace as we raced across the broad porch and down the meadow, strewn with tiny *fraises du bois*, too small to be considered strawberries, and too beautiful to trample. At the river, two sailboats and a Boston Whaler were moored at a languorous dock. It rose and fell in tidal swells, always faithful and always apparent—never doubtful of its duties and never protesting its under-legs of barnacles and moss.

We decided against the effort of raising sails and stepped into the Whaler with its forty horses.

Our daughters looked like dolls cosseted in their life vests: tiny and immobile, a change from their reeling chubby engines to quiet captives. I watched their watchfulness as I bailed out the night's rain water, and primed the outboard motor's choke and checked the fuel tank—each a simple gesture compared to the rigor of sailing: tiller, sheet and lines, mainsail and taut halyards, jib or spinnaker—if you have them—and dropping the centerboard—if you don't have a keel—checking reefing ties, and pointing upwind when releasing the mooring or docking cleats. And the steady predictability of a humming motor was more reassuring than a sudden jibe, or close-hauled sailings into the wind: a broad reach would always be preferable to my wife and daughters—alas!—but today we were bucking waves.

"Daddy! Will we stop to dig for clams?" Sarah begged from her taut collar, remembering we could run the Whaler over sand bars at low tide.

"Yes, and maybe mommy will make spaghetti sauce with the clams."

"White or red?" Lily grinned as the girls pinned themselves to her.

The outboard roared into preparedness, and silenced their answers. Their attention shifted to the upward movement of the hull and the wake spewing behind us in an equal torque as we planed out of Slocums River into Buzzards Bay. We leaned into movement against us, into ourselves, an inverse gravity as the bow pointed into an improbable horizon and we searched from the gunwales to the flattened appearance of islands rising offshore to remind us, Lily said later, of the signposts in our lives. Loving each other that day was a wave of lasting forgiveness—a pledge for life.

All of that is much to take in, absorb into reasonable feelings, when one is bouncing waves at forty knots: the speed alone compresses your emotions into short, constricted breaths. Later, when we beached ourselves in a quiet estuary, my children gathered clams to small red hands, their life vests set aside, and their mother spun tales of hope. She longed for the exceptional life; I looked for the ordinary in which we bless and are blessèd, according to Yeats. We lulled against an outgoing tide as we went home, and the boat sank into its full hull as we found the dock, once again, tied down, and raced for the house the same way we had come. The girls were sleepy, retrieved from any point of excitement.

I slowly realized that Lily was doing for me what I could not do for myself, and helping me step away from the bafflement I had assumed was merely a condition of daily living. As we all busied about the clams and our evening meal I knelt down and gathered my three women in my arms, allowing myself to weep as they bowed their faces upon my lowered head.

"Is daddy crying?" Sarah whispered reverently.

"He's had a very happy day with his girls," Lily kissed

my hair. I remembered what my psychiatrist told me the year Lily's father took her away:

"One day, when she comes back, a sense of well-being will surprise you. Don't look over your shoulder to ask where it came from. It is the onset of living ease, or what the Greeks described as finding something where you never intended to look—I forget their word for it—*aphoria?*"

"Yes, and I did come back!" she affirmed fiercely.

"**—And** it may turn out to be the lapsed beginning of my life," I found myself jumping into Lily's sentiment, which rang as pure and high as carillon bells in their questions and answers simultaneously exchanged. I had at that moment no other redress to my past unhappiness than turning towards her, my lost Lily, who became to me a *pearl richer than all my tribe,* but I accepted as my proper due. "But you must not think me a judge of your character, dear heart, or an arbiter of your freedom to be who you are right now—: I surrender utterly to you and to our children's vision of you, and I'll kiss your toes on that promise for as long as we live—" I stumbled into an abnegation she wouldn't hear—:

"Whoa, cowboy! I'm half of this equation. I owe you my amends—even though you have generously banished them from our life—and I'll always add that measure of fidelity, each day, that we nearly lost."

"I was faithful to you the years you were gone: I hung a lantern in a high place near the roof and waited for you to return. The extravagant gleam of that light watched above the house as the moon could never hang from the sky as a silver pendant—moonlight was shamed in my love for you—and I held that small light in my dreams for three years."

"And now, "she lowered her voice, "I shall return that faithfulness."

"But there will be no place for groveling, my darling: my job is to elevate your life, to restore and perpetuate our hopes when we first fell in love in college—you see, not a moment of our lives has been lost—"

"—and you elevate yourself quite beautifully, and take me high up."

Our easy banter in college days, full of slang and nonsense, had spun itself into a different voice over years. We each spoke cautiously, but in a deeply carved plane of inquiry into every feeling, every emotion, and every moment of intent. This was how we established respect for one another, and set courteous boundaries for ourselves which dissolved in the passion we carried along the years, yet renewed themselves at the break of day, and the breaking of bread at the breakfast table. The girls seemed to find safety in our shifting moods of playfulness and sobriety— an even playing field over whose roused sod they could run endlessly—as they grew accustomed to our various ways of being *available* to each other—and to them.

"You see, my father was never around Sarah much, not available to her every day in and day out no matter what," Lila told me one morning. "He was drowning in that sad rag-heap of once prominent writers-become-screen doctors, and they all drank for inspiration, which my dad never did writing his novels. Believe me, the studio world is degrading!"

"So, he's staying on out there?"

"Once stranded, they never leave—: Fitzgerald, Faulkner, West, Lewis from the days that Hollywood could promise them a last stand, another novel to throw them into the heavens of rehabilitated genius. My father is nearly the last of that tradition—another generation, of course—and his novels became hit movies because that's how they were written in the first place, not as literature but as scripts, and the good fortune to attract Gregory Peck the meager story, yet bustling conflicts in each—"

"You must have gotten a good look at that world, but remember in the end, it's just mere celebrity—it doesn't mean a thing—and the only individual talents are the writers and the directors. Of course the money is grotesquely skewed, like in professional sports, to the celebrities as the roar of approval of half-wits and great un-washed drowns taste."

"Darling," she demurred, I know you're not a snob, but in your New England disdain, you might be seen as a *reverse* snob—"

"—you mean pretending my family is not rich, driving shabby cars and wearing old clothes, and treating arrivistes as if they were less noble than washer-women, whom I revere and have provided annuities for service?"

"That's my man!" she beamed, "although my dad might differ—"

"Well, he's made his bed, hasn't he? Shown his colors—as a snob!"

"What is a snob?" she demanded righteously, coloring suddenly.

"Someone who imitates the manners of the class just above him."

"Sounds like a hopeless enterprise—a gerbil on a wheel? Oscar Wilde?"

"Full marks! You do sound like my grandmother, darling, always a gritty metaphor. In your father's books, they are full of false pretense and gesture—"

"Really, just a glass held up to the 'fifties, full of over-worked irony—"

—"Darling—we need to step down from this high-brow, low-brow bickering We're going to live a fairly simple life with our girls. The past is gone, and neither of us, none of us, has to suffer what happened then."

"How true that is: we've been given the gift of a second reading of our lives, a new look that just might last the rest of lives: Think of it!"

In that song-full utterance, Lily gave me back my life; and every moment since when I have been inveigled into complacency or twinges of regret, I re-capture her words, as I capture her in my arms many times each day. We now have our third child, a boy—a new Fairchild, I am bold to say—; and she has absolved me of a sense of injustice, an entitlement to be offended by the world, or rejected by its vast, impenetrable pretentions—:

"You have your full share of all the world and beyond have to offer," she assured me. "You are not a flawed or incomplete man—wherever that message may have reached you—and you must see yourself as the champion of our home! You guide us, you sustain us and you forgive *yourself!*"

"The message reached me, as you say, when you left me. My parents consoled me and challenged me to forget you—to lose myself at M.I.T.—and I did soldier on for a while. But my center, you, had been taken from me, and of course I am recovering that now, and have our children about me day and night, and have your light back, which sustained me when we were in college and expecting Sarah, and I was going to make a mark in my family's firm and provide for you outside your father's provenance as a collector of human lives in the narrowest sleeve of human emotion—"

"Stop! she pleaded. "I'll not be your therapist! If you need that kind of reckoning, I can drive you over to McClean Hospital in Belmont—after all, it's the oldest in America, founded in, 1820 was it? You Fairchilds must be so proud of that, even in your smug, Quaker restraint—"

"That's where you fail to see where we find the truth, darling. We wait in the silence, and look for the light within—" I offered awkwardly.

"*I am your light within! I am a woman restored to you faithfully!*"

"Bless your heart, I believe you are. I feel pulled back from a ledge."

"And that's where I'll always catch you! At the lip of

your precipice." We had risen to the pinnacle of our long-past winter of discontent: we were stilled.

The girls began to creep into the kitchen where we sat—they had long since had their supper and stories and been put to bed. Upstairs, in their high-eaved room, they must have received an acoustical uplifting of their parents' words below, or magical echoes of what they may have been dreaming in their small beds, the elusive images of sleep which may suddenly, upon awakening, take shape and sound and visual affirmation.

"Mommy? Daddy? We heard you talking in our dreams, and here you are! Is it late? Why are you here so long after dinner? Did we miss anything? Are you going upstairs to your room soon? We looked for you there, because we heard you in the ceiling, and our windows rattled in the wind, and your voices came in through the cracks and we were scared—"

"Sarah, angel, you were dreaming, but in your dream you heard us talking," Lily explained the transference which must have occurred. It was my final frontier, to find our words nestled in our children's dreams. I hoped their soft bedtime exchanges might be present in my dreams, and take a shape of redemption. The girls slept in our bed that night, fast annealed to our curved shapes—Lily on the inside, me on the outside—a chalice I could place my worries and fears for all the days to come.

Very little changed in the coming weeks, and very little took my notice. At summer's end we wrapped our memories in the falling light on the South Coast and made our strenuous preparations to close the old farm and drive to Boston. Each room had to be vacated with a sedulous view of what would be taken away, and what would be left behind to the long anonymity of winter as its solemn understanding of our return in the Spring would protect all in its sleep. The girls wondered what would be the same and what would be different—as did Lila and I—and seemed to know they would come as changelings, offered from one life to another with scarcely a glance at the spirits which would convey them.

Back in Charles Street, all became abrupt and regular. Boston's fine, squared away preparedness for autumn, and closed ranks of various tribes as they awaited winter; the streets and alleyways seemed narrower, pulling themselves from strangers as the business of Boston went indoors. This is not to invoke George Santayana's *Last Puritan*—a near scriptural rite-of-passage for us all in school—but simply present a fond recognition of our habitual natures. Grandmother's house, tall spacious and spare, accepted us four as pilgrims stepping inside for centering prayer, that we may go out on our ships and our ingenuity to conquer a larger world: Lily and the girls could one day walk across the Longfellow Bridge to their school in Cambridge—;

I might take Storrow Drive out towards Route 128 and ignore the Mass Pike; or I could ride the T to Waltham and catch a company shuttle to the Fairchild campus slightly northeast of Wellesley. The former allowed me to pass by the great portals of the Fairchild School, founded by great grandfather Joshua Fairchild, succeeded by his son Mathew, headmaster, who reigned in my day. Then my father Seth, uncle Jocelyn and aunt Lizzy came along and turned their backs on the school's heritage: Seth, off to Paris as a painter; Jocelyn taking the reigns of Fairchild Electronics; and Elizabeth marrying uncle 'Albertine' late in life, producing no issue—another retelling of Tolstoy's *happy families*....

Lily and I have flourished through our years. Both girls went to Brown, and our son Seth followed his grandfather Seth's inclinations to RISD, to study painting and sculpture, and later architecture. His older sisters did try to look after him in Providence, but he soon out-ran their resources as they fell into the social labyrinth of the far bigger campus and he dove deeper into secret coteries of a smaller canvas, yet a wider compass. He turned out a true Fairchild.

Two of Lily's father's novels made into movies—*The Man in the Gray Flannel Suit*,* and *A Summer Place*—as they were essentially scripts, came across better in film than on the page. The first explored the ennui of a WWII flyer as he sinks into the bleak, good gray norm of conformity in the 'publicity' business of 1950's New York, and the redemption of a man through family and good genes. The second portrays two generations of arrivistes and spoiled misfits on the coast of Maine. Both movies reeked of sentimental accommodation despite decent acting.

"Since when has an electrical engineer from M.I.T. become a book critic?" Lily challenged me sharply when I offered this assessment some years after the films and the books had been forgotten—although I still had the copy of Flannel Suit which she inscribed to me when we were in college: Darling *Solly—a first edition! Your Lily, forever at Tufts University.* It was dated 1967, when we were juniors, just turned twenty-one, and I could court her properly with an allowance from my parents' estate. As my uncle Jocelyn, dad's brother, had no children or wife, my twin sister Lee and I inherited half of the Fairchild estate, which would be kept in an irrevocable trust until we turned thirty, after which we might draw full income, and even principle for emergencies or capital acquisitions such as buying a house or starting a business—all subject to Uncle Jocelyn's accord. Lee opened a gallery in Newbury Street; Lily and I got the farm in South Dartmouth.

"I'm not a book critic," I answered her. "I just didn't see the point—"

"What point?" she demanded, as if she were defending a shoal where the sands had already given way to the tides. "It's a story, and it rolls along until it's finished, and then we step away from it, shrug, and if it has touched us in any way we nod, and pull this character or that into a place we'll borrow him or her for a while, and then discard its reference."

"How brave of you—how honorable to defend your abusive father!"

"Does this comment have to surface now?" she wailed. "After these past weeks on the South Coast, when we were in such lovely alignment, day-by-day, with each other and our children. We're married, for heaven's sake, what we so wanted when we left college, and in our vows we said we were blameless for what had gone before! If I forgave my father for separating us, can't you forgive me? —I'm yours faithfully and eternally."

"So you have come to see what 'time without end' is like?" I asked.

"You know the answer to that—don't go all biblical on me—I am incapable of loving anyone else but you for the rest of my life, our life—!"

"It could be a slippery slope, as they say," I teased, feeling release.

My bride laughed to the top of the tall drawing room at Charles Street. "Just like your sister—?"

I laughed with her to the top of the tall stairs to the landing where our children were sleeping but soon came to peer over the oak banisters.

We were on the floor, rolling in each other's arms over the Fairchild carpets from another century, and the children came down the staircase to crawl over us and quickly invent a new game to play with us instead of the one which had brought us to our knees and up to our hearts' blessing.

Lily's father rarely visited us in Boston, and we gave Los Angeles a very wide berth. Saturated with the success of his movies, he found no reason to take an interest in my or her professional lives. Like sad-sack Salinger, he had written nothing more and led a secluded life in the Hollywood Hills. His grandchildren appeared to him as lapsed moments in his life: They were born, grew into teenagers, and fled his vision. I thought, when he first came, to interest him in the lives of wealthy Bostonians who were not Brahmins— not Lowells or Cabots incarnate—but Quakers who prospered sedulously on the sidelines until they became irresistible to the mainstream. I hoped he may find something to write about which would equal the sheltered subjects of his earlier novels: celebrate the under-dog's rise to fame & fortune. But he had long subsumed his imagination in ennui.

"Why should I write anything, if nothing interests me any more?" he asked one night after dinner in Charles Street. "You, dear Solly, can plunge at the frontiers of your science—do they recede in your research, or overwhelm you with their implacable silences—while the rest of us fade away, having done our duty? I'll never get a grant to write another novel, but you'll draw from the government trough and turn corners to escape your final doubts! Then what? Lily is a better bet probing the extremities of art, and I applaud her work in your sister's gallery—at least that direction offers a foundation in human understanding I was never able to provide her—"

"—oh, daddy, you underestimate, or fail to recognize your benefit."

"No, darling: I understand him perfectly. We're better off as we are."

"That's a cruel summary," she protested as I sat quietly in my chair.

"Better that than a sentimental reunion with no foundation of care."

"Care—?" her father shot back at me, suddenly awake to our intent. "I took her from a vulnerable situation, and a predatory rake as we used to call your type, and stabilized a youthful obsession. She gave birth to Sarah safely—" I rushed across the room to face his arrogance—:

"—you need to drop off the map, *pater-in-lexis-eterna!*" I shouted.

Lily dropped into a low swoon, like one of the collapsing women in Antigone, as I recalled, but could not be certain: did Creon admit the presence of women into his demented sanctum? Could Sloan Wilson give his daughter the sanctuary she required to advance into her married life?

I wanted to forbid his presence in our home, in our city of curving lanes and alleys, hallowed in their antiquity, yet accessible as any footpath was for the trudging of the faithful and truthful souls with which Boston abounds, invisible to outsiders: a stout foot bridge or gangway connected our willingness to our halting disbelief, and Lily rose from her supine pose to take my hand as I lifted her into an embrace her father could not have imagined—even in his books—and it was as if lava, from a volcano, lying in its molten repose, decade after decade, had poured over the land from its chalice. We drove him to Logan Airport next day as undertakers.

A sublime calm fell over us as we drove back through the tunnel's yellow lights streaking upon white tile—a wellbeing we could never question even over our shoulders. His sad departure—he seemed not to know what had fallen out of his life—sustained us and drew us into our treasure. "Can it have been this easy?" Lily marveled, a hand on my thigh.

"It's never easy to turn away from a parent," I said, watching our children bouncing in the back seat with little premonition of ever turning away from us. "I never had the opportunity, they were lost at sea, and now are enshrined as gods—or god and goddess—as Lee and I, in our worship of them, are like clay in their hands."

"Then—" she faltered, "I am as free as a bird," her tears at my neck.

"And, to ensure your freedom, I vow to read your father's books again, and watch the movies with a faithful eye," I despaired like a falling rock.

Palimpsest

In Memorium: Gore VidalΦ

I have come across this idea—or can it be a phenomenon?—and found it useful throughout my life. At an early age, in a Boston boarding school, I erased another student's essay and wrote my version of his work. He claimed to have lost it and was given a reprieve by the master to write another. This I eventually appropriated to write yet another layer, to be submitted as a first-year college essay at Tufts: a parchment to success.

I had a Radcliffe girlfriend, two years older—yes, a *'cliffee*—tall and lissome with auburn hair she tossed into an unruly mane, like a chestnut mare. I was her second lover, she my first. Even in those gender-partitioned days we found a small apartment on Wickenden Street in Providence—a mere forty miles from Boston— where she entered The Rhode Island School of Design as I transferred to Brown University. We would both graduate the same year and be married. My plan was to go on to law school. For my LSAT application I revised the old essay from school in a fresh pentimento!

As an art student my wife was very amused at this undertaking, but agreed that old canvases do often need fresh patina. "Actually, darling, you can use these continued versions as a lawyer!" she cried in excitement. "Even your arguments or decisions—should you become a judge—can be based upon all these migrations of your first, innocent theft!"

She, Bonnie Jean Liddell, was of Scots descent, as was I; we were soul mates and fervent believers in Scotland's independence from the moment our lips had first touched and even more devoted when our first child was born and years later we moved to Edinburgh. In between, and when our second child was born, I went to Oxford to read British Law and developed a thesis of precedent based, again, upon my usurped discoveries back in school. I published the entire *oeuvre* of my transcendent work, never my own of course, of twenty years, gathering a legitimate patina.

One afternoon, as I sat in the White Horse with a pint of Guinness and a stack of graduate papers to read, a man my age walked directly to my table. He spread his hands with a confident look, that I might recognize him. He smiled with a generous visage, and said my name. "Evan Payne!"

My name had been taken in vain before, but never without warning; even approaching forty I recognized a face I knew twenty years before, my classmate from secondary school whose paper is now my published thesis at Oxford: "Clive?" I took his hand, which had the soft momentum of regret.

"How did you...come to be in Oxford?" I asked rather than say *find me?* He leaned back upon his heels with preemptive calm and took out a pale meerschaum pipe from his left trouser pocket. "Is that from Turkey?" I nodded familiarly, as I had visited Istanbul a few years before.

"I read *our* essay which you published here. I must say, you've improved on it considerably twenty years later, but the kernel—the soul of it—is there as if lit by a Delphic flame which never flickers! It was also printed in our school alumni magazine—that's where I saw it—and was glad that you had given it new life!"

"Clive, have you come to Oxford to praise Caesar or bury him?" I laughed uneasily, as if trapped by my own prevarication over the years.

"Nothing of the kind! But *Merchant of Venice?*"

"A pound of flesh? How about a bottle of hock from the Trinity College cellar instead?"

"Do you have rooms there, as they say?"

"Two, as a tutor. Do you need lodging?"

"Perhaps for the night. I'm off to Edinburgh in the morning—family matters—; in fact, don't you have Scottish roots? Perhaps we can go together."

There was an assuring cadence in his words, a meter of confined rhythm as in a sonnet: hypnotic yet tranquil; well defined yet infused with vague promise of things seen and *unseen,* as we used to hear in chapel at school: A transmogrified preview of life and fidelity severely compromised, abused, but never put to the test was before us this day.

"Well, there are no living relatives of mine in Scotland, Clive; they all left for the United States in the mid-nineteenth century. What would I hope to celebrate there except a wish for independence?"

"We could unify our own friendship, Evan, and even a kind of brotherhood we achieved long ago in school: thick as thieves and bound like twins!"

I knew then he had inveigled himself into a space we would have to occupy indefinitely, until one of us faced the folly of a copyright or even a shipwright surveying a safe harbor in a storm. We both knew the fury of a nor'easter rounding Cape Cod within a thin November sky, unexpected yet utterly familiar. How I wished our wives were with us to mollify the storm!

"So—we'll search for a deeper past we share, generations layered beneath what we remember?"

I agreed, but wanted to suggest we travel on to the north, to Aberdeen and Inverness, to catch him in the Highlands where I would find safety in the runic remnant of my tribe and there leave him. We would take the train from Edinburgh to Saint Andrews and there rent a car for our further trip.

"Splendid! Let's stop in Edinburgh at Luath Press and see if they might be interested in our mutual dissertation—or variations on a theme!" I knew all my uses—theses, law briefs, decisions—would be brought into uniform light and codified; that Clive would be there as a literary midwife to supervise and edit our creation which, since its publication in Oxford, I wished had miscarried!

Later that night I saw his pipe glowing in the vestibule. The smoke drifted in a spectral stream to meet a small lantern hanging beside the portal to our accommodations. We were lodged on the ground floor overlooking the quad where Oxford's undergraduates stumbled in night revelry—now and then pushing their faces in our window—; I could not at first determine if Clive had noticed me until he spoke, as if to himself, yet directed at me.

"We have begun the vigil I suppose—watchful moments and sleepless nights?" I could not see his face as he spoke, a shadow holding my attention—"Scotland awaits us with its rocks and rills and its haunted history—" his alliteration was hypnotic—"and in its sparse, barren hills find the truth!" The shadow of smoke from his pipe not only concealed his face but his voice as well. I then understood I must take the first train to London and then return to Boston, to an atmosphere and a culture so well diffused and disguised I'd walk the streets in anonymity: like all eternal cities such as Rome and Istanbul Boston sheltered you invisibly.

"We'd best get some sleep," Clive said as he abruptly walked across the vestibule to his room. "We'll have an early start and a very long day—"

I now felt myself a captive pilgrim, set to flee.

Yet I found myself liberated, not captive except by a pendulous delight sitting in the train bound for St. Andrews. I left a cryptic note for Clive that I was returning to London to take a flight back to Boston where my mother had urgently summoned me for a family emergency. I left Clive to guess if it was death or illness that took me abruptly home.

I rented a car, not certain where I'd drive, yet assumed Clive had left Oxford to follow my trail or put his tail between his legs and retreat beyond a ground where we might meet again. I saw that I had the upper hand in withdrawing any power he held over me—I simply stepped aside his heels rocking forward—and allowed him to collapse!

From St Andrews virtually all of Scotland was at my footsteps—I could travel to the Orkneys—: I had a broad compass with which to avoid Clive yet enjoy a freedom I had not known in Boston since I was married. I thought wildly of calling Bonnie Jean to fly over with the children but realized they were still in school: yes, they could make up their exams but separation from their athletic teams would be devastating, as I well knew from my own youth when my father had taken me to France in an impromptu opening of his Rue de Seine gallery.

"We're fine, darling," Bonnie Jean assured me when

I called to explain myself. "You've had your work at Oxford, which is vital—as is the Clive business—and wandering among your ancestors in Scotland will sustain you in your...authenticity? Just be back well before the baby arrives!" She laughed with a generous smirk I could envision even across an ocean.

As we were approaching forty, this would be her last pregnancy, presumably, bringing our nest to an even quartet: two boys, two girls. We'd been only children so we bred freely. She had been a ripe, fecund bride from the moment we met. She became pregnant even when we were students, then three years later; then two; and now eight: when we were thirty we had three children under the age of ten; at forty we would have four. I now ruminate on these numbers, blessed sequences, due to a counting obsession I have carried since childhood—a need to account for every interval in my life—as if what is seen, even unseen, might disappear which a psychiatrist called dissociation.

Indeed, it was calming from time-to-time to view myself as a third person, an outsider looking at myself as a visitor to my own life. Until—

Until what?" Dr. Febiger asked a few days after I returned to Boston from my travels in Scotland, even an exploration of the *Horse Whisperers.*

"Having reached the end I must start at the beginning, as T.S. Eliot said: *We shall not cease from exploration and the end of al our exploring will be to arrive where we started and know the place for the first time—"*

"And what is the 'first time' for you?" he asked as he pulled a *meerschaum* pipe from his pocket: I remembered the pipe Clive had smoked at Oxford, pale blue vapor issuing from his invisible lips. "Or if you prefer, 'the end of you exploring', perhaps the most trenchant line in English poetry since—"

"—Yeats? Coleridge? Wordsworth? Romantics?

"Lets pause with Robert Lowell, close to your own back yard, if you will, and satisfy ourselves that a peaceful moment will arrive when *we* shall revive in our work together.

"Do you mean to draw me back to *Life Studies for the Union Dead?* Am I to take up a sword to defend my heritage and offer swift penance?" Dr. Febiger offered no reply or explanation.

I found myself months later in Walpole Prison, awaiting a hearing in what I though would be an inquest into the death of Clive, who had been discovered in a shallow grave near the New Hampshire border. The authorities knew of our travels, even our quarrel over a manuscript which carried no further meaning beyond a brief and severed boyhood long ago.

"When was the last time you saw this man?" a detective inquired closely. "We found a pistol at his burial ground, not fired. Had your friend ever carried a firearm?"

"Never. When we were classmates at an early age we were close friends. When we married our wives were best friends, and our children grew up together here in Boston."

"Yet we learned of a rivalry you had over a school assignment he wrote and you pinched and years later published in your own name..."

II

A long span of time separated me from where I left my story called *Palimpsest* to an arrival back at Oxford. Nothing there had changed. I sequestered back at Trinity College and within the Bodleian, a blessed labyrinth of manuscripts, precedents and books in the many thousands—a sanctum to find oneself lost, even banished. There I met a woman.

Penelope—I rejoiced in our love-making that she welcomed allusion to a return of Odysseus—was a graduate Classics student half my age who appeared in one of my lectures as a radiant, red-haired Scot who only smiled at my foolishness. My Bonnie Jean had settled in Boston after the death of Clive had been discovered and falsely attributed to me. Despite my exoneration, she, our children and her equanimity required some time apart. As I approach fifty, I realize the separation is captured ruthlessly.

Penelope presented herself a firm, enduring mate who forgave my oversights yet challenged my prospects:

"I canna' love a man, ye must know, wi'no prospects. A home, a child, wi' faith." *I knew.*

$$\psi$$

"Are ye a polygamist, then? What about y'r family in Boston?" Penelope demanded. "I willna' be wife once o'er the fence!" I was charmed by her strict injunction and pulled her into my arms with a kiss to stop her protest. She splayed herself over me with speed and splendor; as her back arched in surrender she cried out my name: "Solomon of the ancients, I shall never be a make-over of previous loves. I shall *never* be a layer or addition to your fidelity. What'er scaffold ye erect, I'll uphold the top—nev'r the bottom: I canna' let ye go!"

She had spoken my name for the first time—a hallowed birthright shared with my twin sister Leah—I commonly called 'Solly', she a simple Lee. I felt a fealty overcome me, a nearness unrestored, never bestowed in the loves of my life; promised only by my mother: "You will find a soul mate, much like me." This covenant has been immured within since the death of my mother at thirty-five led me to build a high wall, a fortress against adversity I had no way of taking down.

"Silly boy," Penelope assured me, "with me you will find that covenant—you already have: I am a mere messenger who loves you eternally!"

"We've known each other not even two weeks and you are my student—wouldn't that be—"

"—frowned upon? I assure you, Boston-boy, there

are no Puritans here anymore! You've them all! What is that famous quote about Puritanism?"

"'The sneaking suspicion that somewhere, someone is happy?'"

"Y'r a happy man in m' hands?" she rolled her 'r' as musically as a rushing mountain stream. "I'm an end and a beginning—"

"—which reminds me of T.S. Eliot's lines: 'We shall not cease from exploration, and the end of all our exploring will be to arrive where we started and know the place for the first time.'"

"'Tis exactly where you and I are—and the twenty-year difference in our ages is a corollary to those lines—: in *media res* of an eternal love!

I felt a shadow fall over my life, a reckoning of *things seen and unseen,* or *done and left undone.* "I do have a family across the ocean—"

"—and did it require Odysseus ten years to return to his Penelope? Plus another ten of the Iliad to wage war against Troy: Even that new feminist translation doesn't emasculate our hero!"

"I read the review in the Weekly Standard by Emily Wilson. It's pretty savage: Odysseus appears a charlatan at best! I guess Homer would blush..."

"But ye must see, m'dear, those twenty years do correspond to our difference in age! Our love was foretold three thousand years ago—at least a foreshadowing, which we must observe and obey."

"I have never been apprehensive over women, as I believe them to be the superior sex: resolved, courageous and compassionate: a man's mission is to listen, never judge; oblige, never offend. A wind of alarm, however, came over me as Penelope gave these ruminations—no, oracular presentiments—in the guise of everlasting love. Even my Bonnie, a fanciful Scot herself, would never preach such a sermon on our marriage. *What's a heaven for?*"

"Aaah, we've arrived at Robert Browning! I warn ye I've the collected works, from *The Ring And Book* to *Men and Women In a Balcony.*"

"I admire your erudition, my girl, as dearly as I worship thy body with mine." I took her in my lap to kiss her even as she began to unfasten many buttons on her bodice, like a rustic peignoir worn over her kilt which barely revealed a roseate knee.

"That sounded like a wedding vow," she softly whispered in a voice from far away and long ago. I saw in her a *peri*, a dancing companion to a peer of the realm in Gilbert & Sullivan days. "We are fixed as *Pelléas et Mélisande* well over a century ago—"

"Bringing Debussy into our lives is appealing, but do you mean we are *doomed* lovers?" I pleaded for her to renounce and withdraw this...phantom!

"*Fated* be the word I suggest. Let's go to bed—there be fires within me that will inflame ye—"

If it be surrender ye want, lassie ye have it."

"Ye sound more and more like a Scot m'love."

We awakened in the morning with a fervent after-flavor upon our tongues and across our loins. Her passion, mounted atop me with ever arching back, gave me the permission to transgress as Odysseus upon Penelope's fidelity. No—I could not slay her suitors—; had she betrayed me, even during these few weeks our...courtship? Assignation? She slept.

I took my phone across to the Bodleian to call my psychiatrist in Boston. We had explored states he described as *dissociative,* where I'd see myself as a third person, hearing my voice as an outsider. Far from depression, or even schizophrenia, this mood was often pleasant, relaxing, reviving even.

"Solomon, it's so difficult to consult with you over the phone and ocean, let alone the siren with which you are besotted beyond reason. Now, I can refer you to a doctor in Oxford—we interned at Mass General—who may shed more light and less glare on your situation. I suggest you come home!"

Penelope appeared behind me and seized my phone. "You were calling Boston! Are you planning to leave me? I promise you it will not be an easy escape. Our vows can never be broken *anywhere."*

One place I could seek sanctuary at Oxford was my former tutor's rooms, away from my room at Trinity where Penelope had easy access: she'd howl in the quad at nightfall, but never would I answer the call: somewhere between Scylla and Cerberus I'd find my resolve—or forgiveness.

Penelope, bless her heart, disappeared upon the vast anonymity of the broad plain of so many Oxford colleges. One night I thought I saw her in the garden at Merton watching *As You Like it* but did not approach her out-stretched blanket—triage I am sure for a younger man—never my pain would compensate for what we had lost.

I left Oxford, my penance to Clive done; Yes he is dead, and yet how can I account for our struggle and the atonement I owe him? Penelope had been a sorcerous, witchcraft in her palms as she raised them in a benediction I accepted as redemption: *A fool, to strut upon such a stage, full of sound and fury, signifying nothing—*

"Shakespeare may be your answer to human personality and mutability; but I have a hold upon your soul for all eternity," Penelope wrote me as I turned my longing to my family in Boston. I left.

The plane, lowering over Boston Harbor, dipped its wings and pulled back from its Logan approach in a sleek, fearful moment: would we land on the water at Nahant, or perish in the deeps of the Bay?

Any misgivings I may have had were eased as I saw,

through the windows, the last of Penelope—a mirage coming to me in the spectral light as we approached the runway—: or a firmament which had embedded itself in my suspended willingness to believe that she was close by, ever near me!

My wife and children were there to meet me, all forgiving of my lapsed fidelity since my ordeal of the death of Clive, yet lingering to a suspicion I could never fathom or accept. I told Bonnie Jean about Penelope and made her accept the brutality of her earlier views—scattered as they were over a doubt we could never overcome or outlive.

"When you accepted the investigation that I had killed Clive, even after I was exonerated, you lost me—no you fled me—: there remains no—how shall say it gently—room for me in your life."

"And our children?" Have you any place for them?" she wailed hopelessly. *Take no prisoners.*

No prayer or invocation could offer a threshold of forgiveness—I came to admit I was corrupt, self-absorbed and wanton in my appetites—: Penelope still held a glimmer of redemption over me; where she may be I had no idea, having abandoned her in the shabby alcoves of Heathrow. Coward! Recluse thriving in my worst instincts become memories! I withheld my emotions in the presence of my wife, Bonnie Jean, and my children there assembled.

"Will it ever be as it was between us?" Bonnie asked

like a penitent before a forgotten shrine. "I am here, with our children. Do you wish to take Penelope as a second wife? I can endure polygamy if you can forgive my precipitate betrayal of you."

"As it was then, in the beginning, it shall be evermore," she cried in a plangent voice I had not heard even during our wedding vows—*vows!*—I longed to hurl at her in a frail retribution: I had no further plea to offer other than penance. Could I turn to St. Augustine, or even Plutarch for relief?

"Your ascendant Classics education at Oxford will not serve you well," Bonnie advised me in her well-moderated voice. "You withdrew from life!"

A pendulum was suspended over our heads as we sought to negotiate—mend our lives together. An exquisite balance was in view which we could not yet grasp; yet the sure faith in the layers of life which unfold and unfold to promise and reveal a new beginning forever stretched upon parchment long forgotten would guide and protect us!

"Did you say something?" Bonnie asked as I gathered her and our four children around me in *un embrasure au mon coeur*—an opening, to be sure—: '*at the end of all our exploration, we shall arrive at the beginning and know it for the first time.*' Phrases from T.S. Eliot recited by Penelope rushed into my awareness I could not repeat for Bonnie Jean. I withheld an immutable devotion to

Penelope and what I had lost in her—: fidelity to an ideal, implacable and never ending, never over.

Penelope, long absorbed in the alcoves of memory, never appeared again, yet I half expected her to appear at Logan Airport with my baby in arms, a phantom who has held an alchemy of longing and regret to this day

The Scotsman Hotel

α

We arrived early at this heavy-hewn, gray-stoned edifice in the center of Edinburgh in time to enjoy a late morning tea with porridge bowl and eggs Royale with smoked salmon. High marbled columns soared above us in a domed canopy over what in days gone by was an editorial room of a near-forgotten paper.

As my ancestors over one-hundred years emigrated from Scotland I felt at ease striding up The Royal Mile to the Castle, stopping by The Tartan Weaving Mill to be measured for a kilt in my family tartan. As Scots is the purest form of English, I was eager to wag my tongue—even to try a phrase in Gaelic—generously returned by all I met—and light my step.

The conundrum of two elevators is another story—as Kipling noted at the end of his brief dispatches from India—as it took days to discover which to get on or off and which corridor led to what foyer. But I could overlook anything in order not to dwell on British tyranny over time from the murder of Mary Queen of Scots to the Battle of Culloden: Naturally my dream, even vocation, is future Independence, at the next referendum.

"Did you say something?" my wife asked as she eased herself into an unusually narrow bathtub. I was swept across over thirty years of marriage to see her roseate, steaming knees held between breasts poised high in an attitude of forbearance.

"Only...the *conundrum* of how small it is in here. Would you like me to slip in beside you?"

"I'd like you to slip *inside* me, if there's room for me on top, *As You Like It,* if you'll pardon my Shakespearean reference—although it's so elegant, so intelligent," whereupon she grasped my swelling integument and pulled me to bed.

"Will you present yourself rearward?"

"Please: that's how our children were conceived, and remains your deepest, hardest regard."

My Gaelic voice has long lapsed, so I could not then offer a prelude or valedictory to our love.
'Yet—I do remember a Celtic marriage vow—:

> *Mile failt dhuit de'bhrweid,*
> *Fad do gun robh thu slan.*
> *Moran laithean dhuit is sith,*
> *Le d'mahaitheas is le d'ni bhi fas.—*

"—and you'll forgive me for omitting the accents in the lines, dear heart, as your forbears came from England I'll leave the translation aside!"

Our lovemaking at sixty is as vibrant as when we were thirty, a decade after we met in college and were married, at twenty and twenty-two. Each moment in bed enriches the next, and beyond any recollection or mere anticipation which may diminish our pleasure we have learned the gift of surrender. "Letting go is not giving up," she said.

We lay vacated of our desire, wrapped in a splendid moment of not knowing where we were or even who we were—an interlude in our lives which offered no boundaries or limitations beyond our love for each other—:

"I can deny thee nothing, any or everywhere—!"

β

The promise was everlasting; yet the shards of truth elusive in the manner of guardians of our legends, legacies and suppositions, evaded the root-bound principle of E Pluribus Unum, unity of purpose and fealty. This affirmation left me week in my knees, not due to soaring patriotism but plangent waters.

"Am I a Scot first or an American?" I asked my wife— "whose name you do yet not know—?" She forgave this and all intervals of impudence, not neglect and mere complacence, easily forgiven—yet rarely forgotten—; "You are my husband, now and ever as we follow and pursue the truth of our lives. We were on a pilgrimage with no compass, steering in dead reckoning, the stars our pendants and the mission upon we embark has no beginning, no end."

"That would be a fair summation of our journey if not for the moments we fell in love again, and sealed our lives and fell into an infinite grace."

"Grace is elusive, if you think about it," she, also named

Grace, replied without ironic hesitation. "I believe it temporal than spiritual: 'In ordinary life, said Yeats, we bless and are blessèd.' A matter of personal worth, if you think of it—"

"What I am thinking of now, darling, is the sheep farm we'll want to buy up north, in Herriot, with four trained Border collies to tend them. It's four hundred acres, gradually hilly with flatlands and quite a good price which I'll not now tell you".

"Why ever not? Is I our anniversary?" she teased.

"We can easily afford it—especially following sale of my family's textile mills in Boston."

"Wasn't that to start up Fairchild Electronics?"

"Yes, but we have investors in California—Intel!"

"Tell me more about the farm."

"The flatland itself swells equally into gentle hills, now you will see covered in purple heather in full bloom. There is a small *loch* half mile in diameter.
surrounded by thick stands of pine. The house itself is a modest manor with four steep gables sheltering the bedroom eaves."

"*Loch*—?"

"A Lake: there are tens of thousands in Scotland, some very deep—"

"How deep is ours? Fed underground or by rain?"

"I haven't yet had it tested: I'd think both, and snow: there's plenty of that in Scotland!"

"Shall we be terribly cold? Can't we spend the winter in Silicon Valley now that you have some business there?"

"The sheep here will take up a good part of the year, whether shearing or lambing. But, m'lass, I'll keep ye warm whether by peat or my flanks!"

"I vow you're already half a beast: you'll as well spend most of the time with the dogs in their special loyalty to their handler."

Ψ

The narrowly rutted way to the farm passed into soaring conifer hedgerows, which overspread the road interspersed by what I imagined to be alder or some close member of the birch family. "The peace here is overwhelming Solomon," Grace whispered.

"It's intimate yet immense. And at our age we'll easily see the differences and similarities—don't you think?" I took my hand from the venerable Rover gearshift to place upon her thigh as, at the same moment, she reached for my member. "I'd best pull over so we may adopt a *slower method* in our lovemaking here in the car. Will it suit you or should we drive on? Mrs. Graves is expecting us for dinner."

"What you are doing suits me beyond measure!" I was securely inside her in a *trice* in the rear seat of the Rover whose cracked leather upholstery in our thrusts gave off a protest of its age and yet an accommodating rhythm. "Oh, my" she cried. "We make love as relentlessly as at thirty!" I had no answer to offer save the moment I was saved.

In the morning we visited the farm manager, who would take us through a sleeve of homecoming—a recompence offered for the years we had been away—: I admitted a chaste surrender that I had fled the near beauty and the far turbulence of dear Friar Angelo as a student in Rapallo; Beatrice appeared before she offered her hand in marriage.

The farm itself was a scant four hundred acres. I measured my years against an expanse I beheld. I had bought my wife to discover this threshold as we were about to cross. As an invertebrate I had no spine to lift me into an upright attitude. She followed me closely as I followed the dogs, ever my renewed companions, prowling for sheep in the hills.

"Darling, you seem more and more absorbed far from yourself—is there something you should tell me—?" Grace asked, her face drawn aside in fear.

"Nothing, darling. I've been to the farm to settle the sale—it's ours, sheep, dogs and meadows!"

"You may be in one of your Scottish moods: I expect you to bark in Gaelic at any moment—"

φ

We left Scotland for Boston in a feral mood: so excited were we in ancestral revelations that we gave our lives over to a Caledonian translation: "If ye ken y'r past, thy future's assured."

"Have we ever been as close or as distant as we are now?" Grace asked me as we sank into first class seats, due to the many miles I had gathered over the years.

"We are wherever we are meant to be—at our age can it be any more simple than that?"

"Yes, absolutely my darling, but there may be a deeper question we have not answered: Where have we been, what have we seen, these many years together? And when shall we arrive?"

"—*We shall not cease from exploration, and the end of our all our exploring will be to arrive where we started and know the place for the first time;* yes, you told me these T.S. Eliot lines long ago"

"Yet we have not traveled, nor are we travelling to a destination I can foresee, as our dogs do not anticipate their futures—nor do I."

"D'st thee liken thyself to a dog?" she asked in a newly found Scottish tongue. "Are ye a mongrel or a thoroughbred? Do ye know the difference, love, or shall I take you, step-by-step, into those flaming embers you have passed by in your life?"

"My footsteps have betrayed yet assured me as I have looked into the barren, futile landscape of my past. You, my darling, gave me a glimpse into the future—: here I see the promised *orb* whose glow offers a heavenly gesture we must grasp."

"Darling, I hardly know if you speak of prophesy or the simple life our lives have taken: I know not the difference, nor care to understand the realms beyond where we stand now: we stand together, bound in future and past, extremities, proximities or the nearness of you and I to our moments, our methods and our *affinities* for goodness sakes—"

"The last time I heard that phrase was grandma:

'If horses were wishes then beggars might ride.'"

Ω

If there were ever an alpha in this story this is certainly not an omega—whatever the signature may imply. I retain this Greek letter to remind me of my duties, fealty and the everlasting struggle this journey has bestowed as a gift upon me. I've scant memories to guide me through a vision I'd not come to trust or obey. Where would I turn?

"An oracle may not carry you far: Whichever you select will offer prophecy or deceit; you decide."

"Shall we have a mentor, to guide and protect?"

'If we are talking about Scottish independence and honor; we shall need play a narrow game—"

"The game, as you say, is merely an image, even a phantom where we have arrived and discovered our lives together; we have arrived and gathered our place in the world we have sought and now imagined where we may wonder—for that is our destiny, our penance and the everlasting, fertile, and promised homeland provided and given in the fullness of time, as the ancients say."

Once returned to Scotland my life as a dog came at subtle intervals; in the end—or beginning!—the transition was final. I saw through a collie's eyes and keen nose to meet those of the sheep with equanimity. My wife Grace, now my handler, abiding my needs and her own—involving Robert the proprietor of Neth Hill Farm with whom she has set up a proper house to draw him from bachelorhood. It seems to have been a good match and I do rely on their superintendence in understanding the sheep and looking to breeding needs of other collies.

"Ye have made a fine home for us darling Grace," I heard Robert call out across the horse paddock one morning as I completed my patrol of the hills and vales of the farm. I have been given a name, Fallon, and promised a mate—.

Now I understand the meaning of *things seen and unseen* we were told in church, and the space an image and a vision occupy across their realms as I recall a phrase from Antoine de Saint Exupery: *L'essential est invisible pour les yeux* and obey.

My life as a dog has been sublime: thresholds never known are in my reach; I enjoy freedom and purity of intent. I am one with my flock and my handler—she who guides and attends to my worldly needs—as I offer a keen awareness and diligence she values. Yet somehow I detect a wistfulness, a longing in her look, as if she would like to recover me as her husband. And as I prowl my assigned grounds, setting my two worlds to rights.

"Fallon! Fallon! I heard my name echo and rebound from the hills. "Come, boy, it's time to go home. Meet me at the Rover and we'll leave today. We have a long drive back to Edinburgh, and I am tired. We'll have to take turns. Why don't you take the first shift, David?"

I heard my earlier, life-long name return as I sat beside Grace, and discovered I was safe in my former life, children awaiting us, excited to hear about my life as a dog, even if to their tender ears it was a dream.